Paradise
MY PRISON

Paradise MY PRISON

George Dismukes

Fresh Ink Group
Guntersville

Paradise My Prison

Fresh Ink Group
An Imprint of:
The Fresh Ink Group, LLC
1021 Blount Avenue #931
Guntersville, AL 35976
Email: info@FreshInkGroup.com
FreshInkGroup.com

Edition 1.0 2023

Author photo by David Pierce
Front cover image by James Garza
Cover by Stephen Geez / FIG
Book design by Amit Dey / FIG
Associate publisher Beem Weeks / FIG

Cataloging-in-Publication Recommendations:
FIC012000 FICTION / Ghost
FIC031010 FICTION / Thrillers / Crime
IC031070 FICTION / Thrillers / Supernatural

Library of Congress Control Number: 2022912565

ISBN-13: 978-1-958922-25-5 Papercover
ISBN-13: 978-1-958922-26-2 Hardcover
ISBN-13: 978-1-958922-27-9 Ebooks

*I wish to dedicate this novel
to my precious soulmate,
Nadine.*

FOREWARD

By Authors RC & JP Carter

Author George Dismukes has had decades of colorful adventures including bull fighting, milking poisonous snakes and handling exotic animals in Africa and Peru. He also worked on movies and in television as a writer, director and producer. These experiences have become a treasure trove for creating novels that come alive to the reader in an intriguing and amazing way. George used his experiences from when he lived in Central America to bring the TWO FACES OF THE JAGUAR Series to life. Shortly after that he wrote the SIREN SONG Trilogy which reflected his love for aquatic adventure and suspense as well.

Now he has written his first paranormal mystery PARADISE MY PRISON. Before you even know Charley Flynt's name, you start to learn about his resolve as a character. As the story flows on, you come to understand Charley and appreciate his honesty. He may have flaws, but he knows what they are, where they came from - and he owns them, often with deep regret. His journey is filled with peaks and valleys and is loaded with unexpected twists and turns. As you navigate his struggle to remember who he is and how he came to be on the island in the first place, you come to appreciate his fortitude and his will to survive.

PARADISE MY PRISON begs the question: What would you do if you woke up on a deserted island with no memory of who you are or how you got there? George's first entry into the world of paranormal mysteries will not disappoint. Settle back and enjoy Charley's journey.

CHAPTER ONE

Awakening

I awoke to the sound of strange birds! Even before I opened my eyes, I knew something was terribly wrong. Instead of hearing the soft hum of my central air conditioner unit, I heard what sounded like small waves washing up on a shore nearby. A salty breeze blew gently against my face. I thought I was dreaming. I had been sleeping deeply. Now, it was a struggle to bring myself up out of that sleep. I slowly swam to the surface of consciousness in an effort to wake up.

When at last I opened my eyes, I thought I was still dreaming! I had been sleeping on my right side, reclining on a small sand knoll that rose up from a beach. I was lying beneath short palm trees. When I looked up, I discovered that they weren't just palm trees, they were coconut palms. And among the fronds of those trees were the birds that had awakened me. They were brightly colored parrots! Several of them!

Parrots? Coconut palms? The beach? Where the fuck was I? I struggled to my feet, clinging to a bole of the nearest palm tree for support, for I was very dizzy. After several moments, in part to give my eyes time to adjust to the light, I looked straight out at the crystal blue ocean. Odd! There wasn't a boat in sight! No oil platforms, no... nothing! Not a cotton-picking thing except water. Blue frigging water, all the way to the horizon! Water!

I also discovered that I was not in very good shape when I tried to turn around to see what was behind me. I was unsteady, confused, muddled. I had to grab hold of the coconut palm harder for balance, then lean against it while I held my head in my hands for a minute. I was trying to shake off an awful, nauseated feeling, like I was falling into a pit, but couldn't hit bottom. It isn't as though I had never had a hangover, Lord knows. But I couldn't remember ever having one to compare with this one. It wasn't just the pain, which was right in the middle of my forehead. There was something very different about it. Had I been drugged? I've never used drugs. I am not familiar with how it would feel coming out from under a drug hangover.

The damned birds above me seemed to be enjoying my discomfort. They made cackling noises that sounded like they thought my situation was funny. At least, the raucous cackling sounded like laughter. One of them even seemed to be saying, "Yum, yum, yum!" Bastards! My head hurt. I didn't need the aggravation of a bunch of stupid birds making jest of my misery.

When I had cleared my head somewhat and regained my balance enough, I did a one-eighty and looked inland to see if I could spot a beach house—or better yet, a store of some kind. Yeah, a store! Maybe I could buy a cold one, or even a six-pack and get back up to water level.

All I saw were more fucking coconut palms and lots of debris scattered on the ground from the palm trees sluffing their older, dried-up fronds. I was at the edge of what could only be described as a coconut-tree forest that went inland for a couple of hundred yards, or maybe more. I couldn't see the other, the 'back' side of the forest from here.

Nothing else was visible. At least, not from this vantage point. So, I backed away from my place of repose beneath the coconut tree out onto the beach. I thought maybe from there, I might be able to spot something else. Something helpful. *Anything* else!

And I did. A very high bluff went up almost vertically for at least three hundred feet. The slope was verdant, covered with bright green ferns and mosses. It was also too sheer for any habitation to be built there. So, I searched the ridge, looking for the silhouette of a building, a house, a store, even a palapa. It didn't matter. I just needed to find some form of humanity, existence other than myself. However, search though I might, I saw nothing. So, I tried yelling.

"Hello? Hellllloooo! Hello?" What I received back was an echo. Me, sounding like me! At this point, even that was a welcome sound. I tried to remember where I had started. Nothing! I couldn't remember a damn thing. I was drawing a blank. I must have really tied one on, to be this amnesic about my evening's activities. I tried harder. But no matter how hard I strained, there was nothing, nothing, and yet again, still nothing. This had never happened to me before. Sure, I had made a fool of myself more than once. But when I woke up, I could at least remember who I owed apologies to. "Gee, Fred. I really didn't mean to knock that Ming vase off the mantle. I am super sorry!" Not even that!

But wait! Getting blasted is one thing. Conversely, these coconut palm trees were out of my territory. We didn't have coconut palms where I lived... did we? Crap! I couldn't remember where I lived. This was crazy! Suddenly, I felt weak in the knees. I walked back beneath the bird-festooned coconut tree and sat down facing the water. I placed my elbows on my knees, my face in my hands. What in the barbequed hell was going on?

I don't know how long I sat there, or why I chose to remain static. Maybe I was hoping the block in my brain would dissipate and let some glimmer seep through. But one thing was obvious, this problem was not going to solve itself. I needed to get up and start walking down the beach until I reached some form of civilization. And hopefully a place where I could buy a beer. I needed a hair of the dog, *really* bad!

When I stood up, something started happening in my gut. I staggered, grabbed a palm bole for support, then bent over and purged. And once I started, it was difficult to stop. By the time it was over, I was pale and felt so weak that I could barely stand. I tried to raise my hand to my head to brush my hair back out of my face, and my hand wavered. I had little control over it. I was so drained and trembling that it was laborious just to complete that simple task. And the frapping birds were still making jest of my dilemma.

"What is so fucking hilarious?" I yelled. "Stupid birds!"

It was at that point that I became scared. My physical strength was compromised. That made me vulnerable to any number of potential dangers. For the immediate, I needed something to replace the wasted fluid that I had spilled all over the sand. And it didn't need to be booze. Truth told, and on second thought, it would be far better if it were not alcohol at all.

Ironic! I was surrounded by thousands of coconuts, each one of which contained some of the best, most nutritious water in the world. And I had no way to get into them. Even if it were possible to hit one of them against a rock, and get past the thick husk, at the moment, I was too weak to do so. That thought added to my mounting fears. Is this where I would die?

And then, that thought caused me to rally somewhat, and realize that I must garner my strength. It would mean the difference between survival or my body rotting on this beach. "The beach turned white with the bleaching bones of dead sailors!" A glimpse! A recall. What the hell was that line from? I couldn't remember.

I needed nourishment, food, something to eat, something to generate strength. But what? Where? There was nothing but coconut trees on this beach. Perhaps, I mused, there might be some other kinds of trees in a more protected area back away from the beach, behind this forest of palms. So, I began to make my way, staggering, through the palms, directly away from the beach. It wasn't easy. I was very weak, and I had to constantly grasp one tree bole after another as I progressed for support. But my survival instinct told me that my life depended on it.

After stumbling around for a half hour, and falling on my ass at least twice, my search was rewarded! I found a huge cluster of banana trees, all laden with stalks of bananas in various stages of ripeness. They weren't the same kind of bananas that I was used to seeing in grocery stores. They were smaller. But no matter, the taste was very sweet, so I plopped down in the middle of the banana forest, leaned back against a banana tree, got comfortable, and ate bananas like a kid in a candy store. I must have looked like a Cabbage Patch kid with my cheeks full of banana!

It didn't take long for the sugar content in the bananas to hit me and steady me, then restore a degree of my strength. Seems like I remembered that bananas are also supposed to contain potassium. More good stuff for the body. And right now, my body needed some good stuff! On the other hand, why was it I could remember what was in bananas, and couldn't remember where I lived, or who I was? The mystery just kept getting deeper!

But I was still faced with the same questions as I had been in the moment when I first woke up. Where was I? How the hell did I get here? Something was so near, tugging at my elbow. But near wasn't good enough. I was perplexed, and that simply wasn't going away. Not yet, at any rate. But it was also not acceptable. I strained harder to recall something, anything at all. It was no use, for now. Maybe in a few hours, or a few days? Days? Oh shit! I hadn't even considered other 'days!' That thought got my attention. And, I turned that attention to my other problems.

Now that a bit of my strength was restored, I knew I needed to focus on my rescue. I wasn't sure how much trouble I was in, but is there any such thing as 'good' trouble? I rose from my cushion of thick banana leaves and walked back toward the beach. My return trip was no more graceful than my journey inland. There were gobs of debris on the ground, forcing me to raise my feet high with each step, then place each foot down cautiously to make sure I was stepping on flat ground.

At last, I reached the place I had started from, with the parrot-infested tree, and staggered out onto the beach. Noticing that the sun was to my left, I turned right, simply because I didn't want to look directly into the sun with my head feeling like it had been caught in a woodchipper. I figured that I had enough problems without burning my retinas. Then, slowly, I began to walk.

I could not shake the feeling that if I walked a mile or so, I would find civilization of some kind. Maybe this place was a tropical version of the Hamptons, where there are scattered expensive houses that in reality are more like estates. I would come up on some elaborately expensive beach house with an old, gray-haired guy standing at the railing on the deck, wearing a sweater tied loosely around his neck and smoking a pipe. There would be some gorgeous blonde with long hair standing next to him. He would see me and take the pipe out of his mouth, using it to point with and say, "Oh, look, dear! There's a beachcomber!" His wife would join him, leaning at the railing of the expansive deck, looking at me and saying, "I don't think we know him, dear. Is he from the Kennedy Compound?"

But one mile turned into two miles, and two miles turned into five miles. There was no sign of human life. None, not anywhere! And still no signs of boats or yachts offshore. No contrails of jets flying thirty thousand feet overhead. No flotsam on the beach, no litter to indicate discarded trash from passing tanker ships. Where in the fuck was I? My worry and fear increased, not because of what I saw, but what I didn't see.

I would have been happy to see anything, even a plastic bottle, or a damned shack on the beach. But there was none, nor were there remnants of any. I looked behind me and saw that the sun was dropping in the western sky. But now it was no longer 'down the beach'. It was inland. That meant that I had traveled in a large curve to the right. Was that just happenstance? Or was I really on an island?

It seemed impossible. How would I have gotten on a fucking island? Shipwreck? I was wearing a white business shirt, dark blue suit trousers with a black leather belt, black leather shoes, and black socks—not exactly the kind of togs one would don for a day aboard a boat, or even a ship.

Maybe a plane crash? Not likely. I didn't have a scratch on me, anywhere. Wait! My pockets! Maybe there was something in them that would give me a clue! I jammed my hands into all my pockets, feeling around for anything. The only thing I had was a cork! It looked like a cork from a champagne bottle. Drat! I was so close to remembering something, but it just wouldn't slide out from behind that thin veil. It wasn't too much of a surprise that there was nothing in my pockets. That is, if I had been at a party. I had a habit of taking everything out of my pants, including car keys and my wallet, and putting them in my suit coat, for security purposes. So, had I been at a party? And if so, where was my suit coat? For that matter, where had the party been?

I continued walking, although by now, fatigue was setting in. I was apparently not in very good physical shape. My skin was not very tanned. I had a paunch. My feet were hurting... Nope. Probably not a denizen of the health spa! It would have come in handy at a time like this. But who knew? Couldn't hardly predict waking up on a beach with coconut palms and parrots!

It occurred to me that the sun was indeed going down. I needed a safe place to pass the night. But where? Anywhere? What choices did I have?

By now, whatever booze or anything else, I had in my system was wearing off. I had the shakes and couldn't stop them. I was also sweating like a whore in church, but didn't know if that was from my poisonous intake or the heat and exertion of this stroll down the beach. Probably a combination—all the above.

The beach was a lot wider here than where I first woke up. There were fewer coconut palms, but many other varieties of plants, most of which I couldn't identify. But by God! I did see a huge mango tree, and it was loaded with fruit. Dinner! Not only that, shade! I made my way to the mango tree and plucked one of dozens of mangoes hanging down, ripe and ready. I had no knife, or other implement, so I had to bite the skin to make a rupture, then peel it with my teeth and fingers. Messy, but oh so good! And I was hungry. My body had already burned up the nutritional benefits of the bananas.

I was not the only visitor to the tree. Dozens of brightly colored parrots and macaws were working over the upper branches, feasting on the sweet fruit. I stayed at the tree for the better part of an hour, until I had eaten my fill and made a complete mess of myself. Under normal circumstances, I would be grossed out at all the sticky mango on my fingers and face. But this day was not normal. I also noticed that this day was within less than an hour of being over. I abandoned the tree to the birds and made my way on down the beach.

I hadn't gone far until I saw a cut in the beach ahead of me. Was it fresh water, making its way to the sea? I hoped desperately that it was and sped up my pace as I neared.

To my absolute delight, I found that indeed it was exactly that. Also hidden from sight when I was farther down the beach was a lagoon, as round as an apple, and as clear as a virgin's conscience. I waded into the cool water, clothes and all. It didn't matter. They were filthy by this time anyway.

I dipped my face into the water and washed away the sticky mango as I drank. The water was sweet, untainted by chlorine or any of the many other sediments from human influence. This washed-out cut through the sand, which was in effect a delta to the sea, was about twenty feet wide, and five feet deep. I waded into the middle and took a bath, even removing my shirt and pants and shoes, tossing them all up onto the bank, where they landed with a wet sounding plop.

The cool water was lifesaving. After bathing and drinking for a few minutes, I just stood there, weightless in the water, absorbing what I could and took in my surroundings. The lagoon was like a postcard in its beauty. It was practically round, surrounded by a beach that ran about thirty feet back to where the jungle framed it. And yes, jungle was the word to describe the tangle of tropical growth. At the back of the lagoon, there was a waterfall, cascading down off the mountainside. Mountainside? Good Grief! Yeah! Mountainside! Because now, there was indeed a high incline that rose several hundred feet!

Under different circumstances, I would feel like I was in a tropical paradise. As it was, I just wanted to know where the hell I was. It would also be damned nice to know how I got here because that would undoubtedly offer a key as to how I would leave.

Forgetting that for the moment, I waded to the far side of the delta, climbed out of the water, and headed away from the ocean beach, wet clothes and shoes in hand. This place was a Godsend. I quickly decided that it is where I would spend the night. I walked a couple of hundred feet back away from the beach to where I found a cluster of banana trees and a large mango tree that would offer food as well as shade. I gathered many of the most green, freshest, large banana leaves to make a thick sleeping pad on the ground.

Damn! What I would give for something to start a fire! A campfire would be just what the doctor ordered. But rather than rue what I didn't have, I was thankful for what I did have. I had water, food, and a safe place to pass the night. Well, at least I hoped it would be safe. I didn't know what kind of critters lived here. "Critters?" Just for an instant... something! But then it was gone. Anyway, that was a huge leg up from how things had begun several hours ago.

So, I settled down for the evening, ate a couple of bananas, and tried to take in the ambient sounds: a distant waterfall, exotic birds, far away shore sounds of waves washing up on a beach, and as sunset drew nigh, the sound of mosquitoes!

Mosquitoes? They emerged from the underbrush with a vengeance and covered me like a black dotted blanket. I killed dozens of them as I swatted, but that was no deterrent. It didn't even put a dent in the Swarm. They continued to attack, nonstop. Within minutes, I was forced to abandon my banana leaf pallet and take refuge in the lagoon.

I submerged my body with nothing but my head above water, and then the mosquitos focused on that!

In desperation, I scrambled back up to the makeshift resting spot and grabbed my wet clothes, then dashed back to the water. I left my pants on the bank for the moment, but spread my shirt out on the water, and covered my head, leaving only a small 'v' shape to breathe through. That helped! It helped a lot, actually! It gave me time to think. How was I going to deal with this new, unexpected dilemma? But then, the problem was solved for me.

When dark descended, the mosquitoes departed as quickly as they had arrived. Oh, there were a few, but nothing compared to the black, biblical plague-like cloud I had been assaulted by earlier. I returned to my bedding place and covered myself with layers of banana leaves, leaving only a small passage where I could get air. In this way, I was able to pass the night in peace. It was a bit too warm underneath all those leaves, which also blocked air flow, but worth the slight discomfort because it offered a shield, free of the marauding mosquitoes.

Next morning. I awoke feeling decidedly better than the previous morning but itching from mosquito bites and a sore back. Not only that, the slight burning on my arms and the back of my neck told me I was sunburned. And now, I was only wearing my wet shirt and underwear. I removed the shirt and hung it on the branches of a nearby bush. It would dry soon. But that was the absolute least of my worries.

I had to figure this thing out. Where was I? How did I get here? What possible set of circumstances could have brought me to this place? And most importantly, what did I need to do next? I did a slow visual pan from left to right. What a shame! It was as hypnotically beautiful as I remembered from yesterday. If only I were here under different, *voluntary* circumstances!

There was the waterfall, only about fifty yards away. It was about twenty feet high up to the fist pool, and maybe ten feet wide. It filled the lagoon with water as clear as crystal. Then there was the delta, the beach, the waves washing up on that beach, palm trees by the thousands, everywhere; their fronds swaying gently, slowly to and fro in the breeze.

And the ocean that was as clear as a bell, unobstructed by... anything! Nothing had changed from my first vantage point yesterday. No oil rig platforms, no passing ships on the horizon. There was nothing! Not a blessed thing! It was as if I were alone on Earth. But of course, that couldn't be. On the other hand, evidence, or lack thereof, would certainly suggest that I was far removed from any human civilization.

So, here were my options: I had a choice. I could either work at surviving this dilemma or I could perish. There simply was no middle ground, no 'grey area'. Survive or die! It was one of two stark choices to make! So, one hundred percent of my thoughts and efforts had to be devoted to that prospect and that alone. Let the other horse feed itself.

With that in mind, the first thing I needed to do was use large stones from the delta to form the word HELP on the beach. It needed to be big—huge, actually. So, I started moving wet stones from the delta and forming the letters. Never mind whether a plane might fly over and see it or not. There were satellites in space with cameras strong enough to spot a flea on a dog's ass, picking his nose. Somebody somewhere was bound to see my message. It took a couple of days to finish that project, for the stones were none too light. But at last, it was done. And now the delta was a little wider and deeper because of me extracting the stones. Meanwhile, the finished word was at least thirty feet high, and just as wide. I felt confident knowing I had done the right thing. "Look, world! I am here! Come rescue my silly ass!"

The next major decision was to decide whether or not to continue down the beach. Either I was on an island, or this was the longest fucking stretch of uninhabited beach in history. From a real estate broker's standpoint, I had walked past untold millions and millions of dollars' worth of prime beachfront real estate. Process of elimination told me I was on an island. Logic told me I was on an island. Every sign and indication surrounding me told me I was on an island. Hope told me I was on a damned long beach and if I kept walking, I would find somebody, some form of humanity, even if it wasn't anything more than an Indian village.

Hope is a crazy thing. It is always the last thing to die. It was the last blessing Pandora managed to keep from escaping from her box. The one blessing that didn't take flight. Hope refuses to ever wane without a helluva fight. It is a double-edged sword because it challenges rational logic. Admittedly, hope is what is responsible for miracles in the face of 'slim to none' chances, or the fight known as 'to do or die.' But it is also the cause for exasperated futility.

As I stood there, next to that beautiful, *safe* lagoon, I knew as sure as birds fly and fish swim that I was going to abandon this secure spot and seek the unknown somewhere farther down that infinitesimal beach. Everything in me said, *don't do it*. But I had to find out. If I was on an island, I had to confirm it. If I was not, I was bound to find civilization and be rescued.

I carefully sun-dried my shirt, pants, underwear, socks, and shoes. Then I jerry-rigged a hat made of banana leaves held in place with twine made by twizzling strands of grass together. Thus prepared, I was as ready as I ever would be. Upon the dawn, next morning, I would venture forth on my safari, and see where it took me. Even though a queasy feeling in my stomach told me that I could not be doing a more stupid thing! A wise person listens to their instincts and heeds them. I was not wise!

CHAPTER TWO

By Dawn's Early Light

Dawn. My third day here. Wherever 'here' was. I woke up hungry. While I was getting a little tired of bananas and mangos, they did sustain me. Under the circumstances, I supposed that I should be grateful. That little voice in my head whispered, "It could be worse!" Think about cows. Nothing but grass all their life. Never once do you hear one of 'em say so much as "Pass the salt."

I dressed and mentally prepared for my sojourn down the beach. I still had strong misgivings about going but pushed them aside. I knew that 'go, I must'. Even though I had a very strong premonition that I would see this place again, it still didn't displace my intention to venture forth on a folly that would come to be remembered by me as "Charley's dumb safari!" I wound up having another couple of choice names for myself too. Stupid asshole was one of them.

And so, I abandoned the lagoon. Everything inside me, every instinct, every molecule was screaming, "You're fucking up, Charley!" But did I listen to that part of me that only had my best interests at heart? Hell no. I did it anyway, damned fool that I was!

I strode boldly toward the beach, wearing my banana leaf hat, the darling lagoon to my left. Once at the beach, looking like Robinson Crusoe, I took one cursory visual check of the vast sea, and the flawless horizon to see if anything might have changed, i.e., sight of a passing ship. But no. Of course not. There were no ships, and absence of flotsam told me wherever I was, I was far-far away from shipping lanes. Dammit! If I just knew what happened, I might get some peace from that. But...

I turned to my right and began walking. The clear ocean was to my left, and the sun was directly ahead of me. East! There were raucous parrots in the palms and other trees to my nearby right who made sounds that seemed like they were taunting me. "Hahaha! There goes Charley... stupid asshole!"

"Who wants to make a bet on how long it will take him to show back up here?"

"I'll take a piece of that action!"

Wait! *Charley?* That's right! That was my name. It hadn't occurred to me to ask my own name before now. Charley Flynt! That's who I am! That's my name! Great! I knew my own identity! Never thought that would be a bright spot in my day, but here, now, anything that represented remembering something took on a whole new meaning. It was a small triumph. Charley Flynt. Now, who was I, really? Who *am* I? I had an identity! I had to have a persona to go with it. "Will the real Charley Flynt please stand up!"

An hour passed, then two. Or at least that is what I was guessing, because, like so much else, my watch was missing. A lightened band around my wrist told me I had worn one. I didn't have my wallet either, or my car keys. Had I been robbed? Maybe somebody drugged me and stripped me while I was knocked out! It made sense! The only blessed thing I had in my pockets was a champagne cork. What was that about?

Normally, somebody drank champagne to celebrate something. What had I been celebrating?

I didn't really think I had been mugged, because why would a mugger move me anyplace? Much less to a tropical place that had to be thousands of miles from my home. No, a mugger would steal what he wanted and leave me lying in a heap.

The sun climbed higher into the sky, and bore down harder. The terrain changed little, nor did the flora. What had changed was my resolve. I was out of energy, out of reserve strength. It was getting hot, and I was reacting to the heat. Then it hit me like a thunderbolt! I had no water. I didn't think to bring any with me. On the other hand, what would I have brought it in? I didn't have a canteen. It also hit me what an amateur I was at this survival stuff. If I wasn't careful, I was going to die, either from the elements, or from terminal stupidity.

One thing had become obvious apparent. This little stroll down the beach was as pointless as it was expensive, in terms of cost to my body. There was or would be nothing but beach. And I needed water to survive. I gave up and turned around. The lagoon was my only hope, it would be my home base until I figured out what the hell was going on.

Hours later: By the time I had returned to my lagoon sanctuary, I was badly sunburned. My groin was chaffed so badly that it was bleeding. My eyelids were badly swollen. I had long since had to remove my shoes, because no matter how careful I was about where I walked, they either got sand or water in them. Wearing them became impossible. But, while walking without them felt good at first, it wasn't long before the sand began to take its toll on my tender, unconditioned soles. This was not fine, sugar sand, but rather, large grained and course.

By the time I reached the environs of the lagoon, meaning the delta, splitting through the beach, I could think of nothing but wading into the clear, fresh water for multiple reasons. My trip down the beach had been very taxing, stupid and extremely unprepared for. The first thing I needed to do was repair and recover from my folly. The second was to not repeat my mistake. Never ever again would I go on safari, wondering what was 'down the beach.' At this point, my body was so damaged that I just did not give a damn what was 'down the beach.' It didn't matter a rat's fuzzy tail, what was 'down the beach.' It was the same old *grass is greener* syndrome. Besides, it was pretty obvious by now that the answer to the question, "What is farther down the beach," is… *beach*! Lots and lots of goddamn beach! Sandy, motherfucking, hot beach!

After a half hour of fighting the current in the delta, I exited the water and made my way back to my encampment of the night before. Progress was slow. My crotch was still on fire! Each step was torture! How could I have done this to myself? Someday, 'maybe' I would be aboard a plane, being rescued, and I could ask the pilot, just for the hell of it, to fly 'down the beach' for a while, just so I could satisfy my curiosity. For now, it didn't make a hill of beans, and I would forget about it for my own good.

Back at camp, I noticed a large rock protruding from the sand with a beveled edge that I thought might be sharp enough to use as a coconut shucker. As much of a neophyte as I was at this survival stuff, I had seen and read stories about the healing properties of coconut. Therefore, my goal was to get inside a couple of them, if it took all day. And it seemed that I had all of a lot of days to do that, or any other thing that would make my existence here a little more commodious!

Finding coconuts that I thought might be the correct ripeness was no chore. They were lying on the ground everywhere. I picked up a couple and waddled my way back to the beveled rock. I grabbed one with both hands and began hitting it against the sharpest part of the rock. After a few inspired blows, the thick husk weakened and split apart. Now that I had a tear in the thick husk, I began peeling it off in strips.

It wasn't long before I was holding a round, brown colored coconut, about the size of a grapefruit. I shook it and could hear the water inside. I knew that if I just broke the shell open, the water would spill everywhere. But what else was I to do? I didn't have any tools. So, I got prepared by sitting on the ground adjacent to the rock. I began tapping the coconut against that rock. I was ready, with mouth open to hold the coconut above my mouth and get some of the nutritious water the minute the shell cracked. I hit it several times, increasingly harder. At last there was a breach in the coconut shell. I held it above my mouth and drank. A lot of it spilled and went down the sides of my face. But I was lucky and caught quite a bit of it. Delicious! Would it be worth the effort to repeat the process? Yes indeed!

Then I cracked the shell open the rest of the way to reveal the milk white coconut meat inside. By working at it with a pointed stick, I managed to break quite a bit of the meat loose from the inside of the shell, and had a meal. Coconut fresh out of the shell tastes nothing like copra, the dried, shaved version one buys in the grocery store. This was curved in shape, white meat with a thin brown coat. It was crunchy, like chewing almonds, and oh so delicious. And from what I had read, one of the most nutritious things in the world for you.

It also represented another food source! It would be nice to eat something besides fruit for a change. Besides, every additional food source that I had improved my chances of survival until rescue came. Rescue! Rescue? How many days, Charley? How frapping many days? Never in my life had I wished more for a crystal ball to see what lies ahead. But something told me, whatever it was, I would endure it, albeit alone. The positive instinct in that feeling was that I would 'endure'. I wasn't sure how, exactly. That would come one moment at a time. That was my status and must become my philosophy; *one moment, one step at a time.*

Then, the uncertainty rushed in to try and obliterate my confidence. How long would my luck hold out? I was vulnerable against almost everything. What if I broke an arm or leg? Even a small wound, such as the chafe in my crotch, could have serious consequences. I could mash a finger or two, trying to bash those coconuts against the rock to burst them open. What if I cut myself and couldn't stop the bleeding, or what if the cut became infected? Even an infected tooth or something as minor as a stubbed toe could do me in. No available medical services meant complete exposure, vulnerability to any and all considerations.

There also weren't any modern, well stocked pharmacies here, where I could visit and purchase any over the counter wonders. Suddenly, I felt very naked. Even a tick bite could give me some kind of fever and do me in! I saw a news story about a woman who developed an infection from a tick bite and had to have her hands and feet amputated. And she wasn't on some desert island. She was on vacation with her husband!

Hypochondria? Under normal circumstances, perhaps. But these were not 'normal' circumstances. To me, it sounded like a self-admonition to take all precautions and avoid folly such as the one I was hoping to recover from.

Then, I shook my head, and it reminded me that I still had my banana leaf hat on. Okay, so, mental note: Be cautious in all that I do. But I could not and would not live my life in a constant state of fear. That isn't living at all. I vowed to keep my head up and my eyes straight ahead. I would survive 'this.' I would ride this horse to the end of the trail. I told myself, there had to be an end to this bullshit somewhere up ahead... right? Focus on that! Focus on the positive. Even a PMA would improve my odds.

Now! That issue was settled in my mind, I needed to turn my thoughts to other priorities, such as feathering my nest, as it were. If this spot beside the lagoon was going to be my home for any amount of time at all, I was going to make it as comfortable as possible. Feather my nest, as it were.

So! What was possible? I had no tools. I had no makings to do anything. Therefore, what could I assemble using just my hands? A lean-to would certainly be in order. But for that I would need sticks. I had no sticks, and no ax to cut any. I also badly wanted a fire. But I had nothing with which to make a fire. I hadn't been a boy-scout, so I had no training in the rubbing the sticks together technique.

Where there was a will, there had to be a way! I left the clearing and made a path through the underbrush, seeking saplings small enough that I could break them off with my hands. They weren't hard to find. Breaking them off was another matter, because they were too pliable. So, I pulled them up, roots and all. The soil was almost all sand, so it wasn't too hard to do. Materials were abundant. Skill might be a little lacking, but the mother of necessity would, hopefully, smooth over that gap.

By evening, I had created a structure, as such, with an arch shaped opening using saplings, the ends of which were buried in the sand, to hold them in place. From that archway shaped opening, I had affixed poles slanting back eight feet or so, where they rested on the ground. Then I tied cross branches, thereby creating a grid, capable of supporting a cover made of banana leaves. At least for the moment. I knew the banana leaves would dry and be useless after a day or so. But for this first approaching night, I felt good about my new lean-to. I also cushioned the ground beneath it with several layers of fresh banana leaves. After that, I waded into the lagoon to wash off the sweat. My hands were sore and bloody. I wasn't used to this kind of labor, and my hands were really paying the price. They would suffer. Then, they would toughen and become calloused with time. They, and I, had no choice.

The cool feeling of the water was a tell-tale indication of the sensitivity of my skin's condition. I was sunburned, and it was starting to hurt. Then it hit me like a lightning bolt! An incredible sadness came over me and I began to sob. I did not understand why I was so melancholy, although I suppose I had plenty of just cause. But I stayed there, in the water of the lagoon for several minutes and purged. By the time I slowly waded out of the lagoon, I felt spent, weak, defeated. I went straight to my lean-to and covered myself with a blanket of banana leaves, without stopping to forage for anything to eat. I was sick to death of bananas anyway.

The 'not knowing' was getting to me. The complete absence of memory was torturing me. What possible circumstance could have brought me to this place? What happened to my life? What *was* my life? I drifted to sleep, confused, consternated, and totally exhausted.

CHAPTER THREE

Exploration

I felt a little better the following morning, although I still felt an unexplainable sadness. I was rested, but no less puzzled. I stood in front of my lean-to, looking around to see what might be new. There were many seabirds frolicking on the beach, chasing little crabs, or something. The birds might be good to eat. But I had no way to catch one, much less cook it.

I decided that if I was going to be a captive here, then I could at least be captain of my prison. Keeping that in mind, I still felt the first thing I needed to do was explore my realm, if for no other reason than to discover what other raw materials, and/or food sources I might use to improve my situation. I had done the 'down the beach' thing and that had proved to be counter-productive; well, actually, nearly disastrous, in so very many ways! Mental note: pay attention to that little voice in my head when it's screaming, "You're being stupid!"

I looked around and focused on the waterfall. That waterfall was being fed by a stream from somewhere. Perhaps that is what I should be exploring. At least I would have fresh water available, no matter what may come! I put my clothes on and headed for the left side of the waterfall, where it looked like I might have a chance of climbing up, over the bluff, using some dangling vines as ropes, to ascend and begin my adventure.

By clinging to vines and the trunks of small trees, I did in fact gain access to the top of the bluff, and a view of the stream which flowed lazily down the side of the mountain. What I saw took my breath away! There was a large clear pool here, which overflowed into the waterfall. The water was so clear that it was like air. I could see fish swimming several feet under the water and halfway across the pool. It was like looking into a very large aquarium, so impeccably beautiful that it seemed artificial.

I turned and looked upstream. The scene before me was a postcard. The beauty was such that it defied description. It was hypnotic. The stream was flanked on both sides by flowering trees with a riot of vivid colors. There were huge trees here, many of which bore fruit. I recognized one as a tree I had seen in multiple movies. It was a breadfruit tree. It was huge, with large, broad leaves and laden heavy with breadfruit, bigger around than coconuts! Voila! Another food source! Next to that was what I thought was a wild fig tree, but the figs were high up in the tree. I would have to climb to get them if I wanted them badly enough.

Many birds were here, including a very large one with a black body and a golden colored beak and head that I had seen in zoos. It was a hornbill. A hornbill? Wait! Everything I saw raised more questions about where I was. I didn't remember much about my zoological interests. But it seemed like I remembered hornbills being from some part of Asia. On the other hand, many of the parrots I saw, and particularly the macaws are new world birds! What the hell?

Cautiously, I took a step forward, because the beauty was such that it seemed artificial. I wasn't sure if it was real at all, or if I was dreaming. Things such as the birds from mixed continents reinforced that concern. Meanwhile, I was distracted by sweetly scented air wafting upon me to complete this living fantasy.

An hour later: Each step I took was like turning the page in a full color coffee table book, a laurel-wood dream where every detail was perfect. There were no flaws. It would be easy to hit emotional over-load here, to become so mesmerized with the place that a person would never want to leave. Only, the grim reality of my situation kept yanking me back. But man-o-man would I have a tale to tell when I was finally rescued! There is no way anybody was going to believe me when I told them about the beauty of this place! Why didn't I have a camera, or at least my phone, which had a built-in camera? It was also among the missing items.

I continued on up the mountainside for another twenty minutes, fol-lowing close beside the stream where there seemed to be a natural path. And then I saw it! There, on the left, up ahead about a hundred yards, up above the stream, in the side of a rock wall. There was a large open-ing that looked very much like the entrance to a cave. I felt goosebumps! Why goosebumps? There was nothing spectacular about finding a cave up on the side of a mountain.

Be that as it may, I had to go to it, go inside it, at least a few feet and see what was there. I worked my way carefully toward the cave entrance, climbing upward along a very narrow path. It was in a steep wall of the mountain, so it wasn't all that easy to access. I was surprised, to be using not just a path, but what looked like an old path leading up to the mouth of the cave. It was narrow, trepidatious, and weed covered. Safe only for mountain goats. But by using it, the last few steps to my goal were made possible. Of course, it would have been easier had I actually been a mountain goat!

But then, there I was, face to face with the mouth of the cave. A few spider webs draped the entrance, which I quickly brushed away with a handy stick lying nearby. There was one huge, very colorful spider that looked like I did not want to mess with him. But he scurried away. He apparently didn't want to mess with me either!

I made the final step from outside the cave, to the sandy/dirt floor inside of the cave. It seemed to go back about thirty or forty feet. It was symmetrical in shape, like a pipe instead of tapering. Starting at the mouth of the cave, it was about twenty feet wide, and fifteen feet from floor to ceiling, and maintained that headroom consistently as it deepened into the side of the mountain. The soft sound of the stream made an echo in here.

It took a minute for my eyes to adjust to the dim light, but then I started to see things. There were a couple of boulders situated toward the back of the cave, and more or less in the middle. Then, I began to notice other things, starting with what looked to be a human skeleton! I crept closer. Could I believe what my eyes thought they saw?

Yes! Closer inspection confirmed that it was indeed a human skeleton! He (?) must have died lying on his back, possibly leaning against the boulder to prop himself up. There were remnants of a campfire nearby. Poor bastard. What were the circumstances that brought him here? What did he die of? About a thousand questions hit me at the same time. It was a strange relief, because it gave me a chance to think about something, or somebody, other than myself, and my own misery.

Perhaps I might get answers to one or two of my questions, 'if' I was lucky. Then I saw evidence that might have been a leading cause to this person's demise. His left femur was shattered. Had he broken his leg on that mountain goat trail, trying to gain access to this cave? If so, without medical help, his fate had been sealed. I had visions of him agonizing, feverishly, in too much pain to provide for himself. Unable to gather food, or even go for water, which was only a hundred feet away, he would have slowly perished, died in an agonizing fever. Good Lord! What a horrible way to die!

As I stared at him, I found myself saying out loud, "You poor bastard! Who were you? What the hell was it that brought *you* here?"

He had been wearing glasses, but of course as the flesh rotted away, they had fallen from his face into the soft dirt beside him. I carefully picked them up. They were in remarkably good shape, but a very old style, wire rimmed. Everything about them, even the wire was in pretty good shape. I tried them on. They weren't my prescription. No surprise there! Then I had an idea, and I was more than a little excited by the thought. With these glasses, my campfire problems may well be solved! I smiled, then folded the glasses and placed them carefully in my pants pocket.

Encouraged by this fortuitus discovery, I began to look carefully around the rest of the cave. It was a good thing that I did so, because it was a bonanza! I quickly found an old, broad-bladed cutlass, like the ones you see in pirate movies. Who was this guy? Well, more accurately, who had this guy been? Had he been ship-wrecked? Was he a mutineer who had said 'fuck it,' taken to the sea in a lifeboat, not realizing how far he was from… *anything*? Then, he wound up here! Maybe the lifeboat sprang a leak. My God, the possible scenarios were endless! But when it came down to it, the only important chapter was the last one. Somehow, he had wound up on this island, made his way upstream to this cave, which he apparently used at his encampment, broke his leg in some gruesome accident! And because of that misfortune, he had suffered an agonizing death, here, far away from the rest of the world. Alone! Totally fucking alone! No family, no friends. Not even a dog, most likely.

A dog! A dog? I had a flash, but no. I forgot about it and continued the business at hand.

Looking at the old skeleton was a stark reminder that if I didn't want to wind up lying beside him, I needed to take every precaution possible, and never let myself forget this image, even for a second.

Why had he come here, to this cave, anyway? I suppose the cave would have been a strong shelter from storms. Food was abundant… if you were a vegetarian. But by recusing here, he was abandoning any hope of signaling a passing boat, or ship, and the possibility of rescue.

Or, maybe he didn't want to be found! Maybe he was a fugitive, hiding! Had he been on the run? An escapee, a convict? A criminal, a pirate? A fugitive! My head was spinning with the possible scenarios.

His clothing would suggest not. Not much was left of them. They were rotted, mostly, but his pantaloons and blouse would suggest that this skeleton was very old; at least one hundred years ago, maybe more. They looked like something an old sailor would have worn. Maybe he just ventured here and stayed because it seemed the safest place to him at the time. Were there lessons to be learned from him? The only lesson I saw was that broken leg, which I was willing to bet he got from slipping on that goat trail out there, like maybe in a rain-storm. I guessed that was a good enough lesson for now. The longer I remained in this place, the stronger my survival instinct became, as well as my absolute determination to not befall the same fate.

I departed the cave. There was more exploration that needed to be done here. But for the present, I felt like I was escaping with valuable treasures; the eyeglasses and the old cutlass. I made my way very carefully back down the goat trail to the edge of the spring, then decided to return to the lagoon. There would be other days for further exploration. And it seemed that I had plenty of time to do that!

CHAPTER FOUR

Charley Town

My amnesia was preventing me from remembering who I was. Well, that is, anything more than my name. I could not remember my background, or what I did for a living, or where I was from. But I could remember how to do things. Case in point was to gather various flammable items to use as punk and mash them together. Palm fronds have a wonderful fiber at their base, resembling loosely woven cloth that is perfect for the purposes of fire building. And so, I was able to assemble the materials necessary for the beginning of a fire. The sun provided the only other essential that I would need.

I held the eyeglasses in place, not unlike a magnifying glass, focusing the beam on the punk. It took time, but after a while, a small plume of smoke began to curl its way upward. I nurtured the start by blowing gently at the base, where I had focused the beam of the eyeglasses, until finally, a small flame appeared. Within the next minute, I had a fire going, and began adding larger wood. I smiled. But I wanted to yell out loud at this major triumph! A fire was indeed a triumph, and as necessary as it was ancient. Even cave people made a giant leap forward when they learned how to make fire and put it to work for their purposes. I wondered if they had felt like I did in this moment.

In celebration, I climbed over the top of the waterfall and made my way to the huge breadfruit tree, where I plucked two very large, greenish-brown breadfruit. I was going to eat something besides bananas for dinner tonight! I had never eaten breadfruit. But I had seen films where people cooked it by placing it into the coals of campfires. I would do the same. I wasn't sure how long to leave the breadfruit in the coals. I would have to experiment, to learn by practice, play it by ear. But now that I had the means to make fire, and a source for plenty of breadfruit, I was sure that practice would make perfect. I could afford mistakes, and I was good at that!

As night approached, I sat comfortably atop fresh banana leaves beside my campfire. I now felt less apprehensive about my chances of survival. There is something very reassuring about a campfire. It is easy to understand what Neanderthals must have felt millennia ago. I wondered what they might have talked about as they sat around the fire at night. Or did they bother to talk at all? Maybe constant social intercourse wasn't necessary in those days.

I had burned wood to make coals, and then placed one breadfruit upon those red-hot coals. Guessing, I left the breadfruit untouched for about ten minutes. It looked like the outer skin was beginning to turn black, so I used large sticks to roll the breadfruit over one hundred and eighty degrees. It stayed there for another ten minutes, then I rolled it out of the fire, onto fresh banana leaves. I used my new cutlass to slice it open, top to bottom. Steam issued from inside of the breadfruit. I used the point of the cutlass to dig at the flesh inside the breadfruit. Tentatively, I took a bite. It was incredible! It tasted remarkably like fresh baked bread. So much so that I wished I had some butter to slather on it.

What I did have, because of this triumph, was an additional food source. It was cause for celebration! I ate my fill, bathed in the lagoon and bedded down for the night, watching the campfire dwindle into red coals. With luck, a few would survive until the morning, and I could rejuvenate the fire by adding more wood, without need of the eyeglasses.

I awoke the next morning feeling invigorated. I was overcoming the life threatening challenges of my new world, slowly, but surely. I did a quick check and found that indeed, there were still lingering coals alive. So, I added more wood, and within minutes had my campfire blazing. I felt reassured. I would continue to add fuel to the fire all day, building a deep bed of coals.

The next thing I did was take my morning stroll to the beach, there to look around, hoping to sight a ship. Of course, there was none. That was a disappointment, but not unexpected. I then looked skyward in search of any tell-tale con trails. Nope! Now that I had performed that errand, I could turn my attention to other things. I grabbed a handy palm frond and used it as a broom to brush off my HELP message on the beach. Then, looking around and seeing nothing else that needed attending here, I returned to camp.

There, I kept thinking about the old cutlass. I had a tool! I needed to make the most of it. I would begin by improving my living conditions. I was not an animal. I refused to live like one, now that I had the means to change that! I seized the cutlass.

Number one on my list was, I was tired of sleeping on the ground. It was uncivilized and downright uncomfortable. But there was no room in my lean-to for a cot. That line of thinking progressed until the truth became obvious. I was going to need a hut, not just a lean-to. A hut! A large hut!

The idea made me smile. And now that I had this wide bladed cutlass, I had the means to cut small trees and bamboo for the framework, and to cut palm fronds for a roof and siding. I got excited just thinking about it. An actual structure! The implications were incredible!

I had an image in my mind of a hut. Basic, but functional. I started by finding a stand of bamboo, and began cutting pieces that I would use for the framework of my new home. That wore me out! Cutting bamboo is not easy. A saw would have been better. But I was in no position to argue. I cut bamboo poles for a full day. I had to take frequent rests. But by the end of that first day, I had a nice stack of poles that I estimated would be enough for the framework. If not, I knew where to get more!

Now I needed to pick the 'just right' location for my hut. I pulled back from the edge of the lagoon by about fifteen feet, then planted four corner posts in the sand, about eighteen inches deep. Then came the cross members, which I tied in place with twine, which (again) I twizzled from grass. I worked hard to make sure the framework was as strong as possible. I decided, in my exuberance, to attempt building an 'A' frame roof. Completing the framework for that idea was a trick, but I got it done. I had to construct a rough version of a ladder from bamboo to get as high as I needed, to work on the roof. Then came the roofing and the siding, all made from palm fronds.

It took eleven days of non-stop work. But at the end, I had a hut, ten feet wide, ten feet long, with 'ceiling joists' and my preferred 'A' frame shaped roof, shingled with palm fronds. In reflecting on the project, my search for materials, I had managed to come across a stand of reeds that came in very handy for tying things together. That solved a lot of problems!

Then, I set about building a wide cot to fit inside my hut. I constructed it entirely from bamboo, lashing the various parts together with twine which I made from reeds. Then, I padded my cot with several layers of banana tree leaves. I knew I would have to replace them every day or so, but that was fine. Goodness knows, there were enough banana trees in close proximity. At least I would now sleep eighteen inches off the ground. It was no small triumph.

Moving into my hut was like moving into a new house. I was proud of my hard-labored accomplishment. I had constructed the hut so that the door would face the beach, and I had built a window into the rear wall on the opposite end. I had harvested and split palm fronds for roofing and siding material. Would my roof repel water? Only time would tell. But I had done my best to layer the fronds in a shingle fashion. What I had in reality, was a hut with a palapa roof. To me, from this perspective, it looked like a castle! Ah, yes, call me a dreamer! But when a person awakens to puzzlement and fear, and then begins to overcome life altering circumstances, things take on a whole new perspective. A new depth of meaning. Things which a person normally takes for granted are not so here. It is a good lesson in life. That is definitely a good thing. It also revitalizes hope in a very real way. One is assured they are not deceiving themselves in an effort at false bravado to keep reality at bay. I looked at my lean-to, only yards away, and thought of it as "The Old Place." How odd!

I stood in front of my new hut and had a small ceremony. Feigning the sign of the cross, I said loudly, "I hereby name thee, CHARLEY TOWN!" End of ceremony. I never was very big on pomp! But I did stand there for a time, smiling at my new home. Be it ever so humble!

Many ideas had come to me as I was busy, building my hut. I had seen fish schooling in the lagoon almost constantly. But I had no way of catching them. Even if I fashioned a fishing pole, and I had plenty of bamboo to do that, I had no line or hook. Much less anything to use for bait. Then, I thought of a trap I had seen in a sporting goods store. It was made for catching minnows. The design was simple enough. A tube with an inverted funnel shaped end. If I could build a hut, certainly I could build a fish trap. And so, I set about doing exactly that. It turned out to be an all-day project, but at last I had the possible means to catch fish, and thereby add another food source to my diet. I weighted the trap with a couple of rocks and placed it in the lagoon near the delta.

The day had been long, but rewarding. Now, I built up my fire, gathered a couple more breadfruit from my 'market tree', and bathed in the lagoon, in preparation for my evening. Later, as I dined on breadfruit, I thought of the breadfruit's history.

In 1787, Captain William Bligh had been dispatched from England, on a mission to Tahiti in command of Her Majesty's Ship, Bounty, to gather breadfruit plants and transport them to Jamaica, where they would be grown to feed slaves. In 1789, the shit hit the fan on that voyage, because Bligh was a mean bastard and his crew mutinied. But then, damned if the British Admiralty didn't 'punish' Bligh by giving him another ship and telling him to go back to Tahiti, and do it right. "And, oh, by the way, better ease up a little bit on your crew this time. It could have been worse!"

That second voyage was one of the greatest success/failures in the annals of history. Bligh completed his mission. The sapling trees were successfully delivered and transplanted in Jamaica, where they flourished. But when the trees got big enough to bear fruit, the slaves didn't like the taste of breadfruit and wouldn't eat it. They weren't used to anything that tasted like bread. Guess there just ain't no accounting for taste!

Oh! And here's a really ironic twist. Following his second voyage to bring home the groceries, Bligh was assigned to a prison in Australia where he was put in charge! "The warden!" Yep! They made him a warden and gave him carte blanche with the lives of dozens, perhaps hundreds of men! Guess England decided to make the most of Bligh's natural talents!

Ironic! If I could remember that historical trivia, why the hell couldn't I remember who I was? I mean, 'really' who I was/am? My identity? Where was I from? What had my life been like? I went to bed, full, but frustrated. I listened to the sounds of the night frogs, and they sang me to sleep. My new bed was a vast improvement from sleeping on the ground.

CHAPTER FIVE

Return To the Cave

"You're a real motherfucker, Charley!" The woman's voice was loud, almost screaming! And filled with venom. I came up off of my cot in a start and rushed to the door. But no one was there. It was the middle of the night. The frogs were chirping happily. The moonlight silhouette of the palm fronds revealed that they were swaying gently to and fro very slowly. The moon overhead was bright, and in a clear sky. The light from the moon was casting shadows of the palm trees against the sand. My campfire had burned down to embers, revealing that it was late night. I was as completely alone, as I had been.

So where had the woman's voice come from? Had I dreamed it? That was the only explanation. I had to be dreaming. Wow! What a dream! Why would some woman be calling me a motherfucker? Could this be the beginning of recall? Could my memory be slowly coming out from behind that fog? If so, I hoped it was a good thing. Being called a motherfucker wasn't a very positive beginning! "Motherfucker!" What had I done to inspire such wrath?

I did not get any more sleep that night. I lay awake on my cot, eyes wide open, trying to put a face with that angry, yet familiar female voice. To say it had been accusatory was an understatement. Punishing? That too. What could I have done to infuriate someone to that degree?

Eventually, by dawn, I drifted off. Blessed nothingness wrapped me gently in its arms.

So, when I was awakened, not too much later, I was not happy. A bunch of birds, including parrots, were having some kind of spat in a nearby tree. All sorts of hell was being raised, so I walked to the base of the tree where the birds were engaged in a battle up in the branches of the tree. I looked up, curious, squinting.

It seemed as though some kind of bird, which looked like a raptor of some kind, was trying to raid the nest of some parrots. Apparently, there were baby parrots in the nest, which the fish-hawk, or whatever it was, wanted for breakfast. This resulted in a pitched battle, the adult parrots defending their young with their lives. This was no minor spat. Life or death was at stake.

The hawk had actually managed to pull one baby parrot out of the nest, and was holding it in its beak. But one of the adult parrots had the hawk by the leg and was biting down with all its strength. There was a lot of wing flapping and vocalization by all of the birds. Finally, the raptor capitulated, dropping the baby parrot and pecking at the parrot who had a death grip on its leg. It pecked hard and long enough to break free, where upon, it quickly flew away, squawking in pain and defeat.

The baby parrot fell down through the branches of the tree, bouncing off of a couple of them and landed with a plop near my feet. I knew it was doomed, because birds, even parrots, don't have the means to grasp their young and return them when they have fallen from the nest. And so, I gathered up the small bird and extended my index finger, to offer it a perch. It accepted the gesture, and sat there, trying to fluff its feathers and preen, after it's near-death experience. It was a baby. Therefore, it did not make the usual 'grack' sound that adult parrots make, but rather a sound that reminded me of someone drinking something and making a glugging sound, or trying to start a lawnmower engine.

One thing was for sure, it was hungry. All little animals have one priority, to fill their bellies! But what was I going to feed it? I didn't know what baby parrots ate, save for possibly, seeds. Banana? Would the little critter eat a banana in a pinch? I found a temporary perch, fetched and peeled a banana, broke a small piece off and offered it to the little bird. It accepted it. I offered it another bite with the same result. Ha! I was a bird rescuer!

Meanwhile, the parent birds had climbed down to a lower limb in the tree and were watching me closely. They seemed to show no fear of me and then it occurred to me; they had never seen a human being before now. I did not appear to be aggressive to them, so they felt no need for fear. It was a strange feeling to be 'the first' human. Would all animals here react similarly? Most likely.

For now, I had a pet, like it or not. I had adopted a parrot! So, I Jerry-rigged a perch for the baby parrot, in front of my hut. I planted two poles in the sand and connected them with a cross bar. I managed to make food and water cups out of coconut shells, affixing one to each end of the crossbar. The perch wasn't perfect, but the parrot didn't complain. I gave him water in one cup and filled the other with pieces of banana. He was a hungry little rascal. It was going to be a challenge to keep him filled up. So, I named him, Phil!

As I stood in front of the new perch, talking to my new pet, I got a big surprise. One of the parent parrots flew in and landed on the perch, then proceeded to feed her baby by regurgitating food into its wide opened mouth! This was unexpected help. And it was gratifying. I had been accepted by this little parrot family. Wow! Suddenly, I was a parrot pal. It was a great feeling! A genuine connection with nature. Then again, something tried very hard to take shape in my memory. It was a flash. Then it was gone.

Now that I was a responsible parrot parent, it occurred to me that it would not be good to leave Phil outside at night. So, I set about building another perch inside the hut, where he could safely pass the nights. I duplicated the outside perch, complete with food and water cups.

So... I had a pet! Or possibly more than one pet. I was not alone anymore. There was a life that I was responsible for, and it was a good feeling that is hard to describe, even to myself.

I had been so consumed with the parrot that morning, that I had not taken my stroll to the beach to do my ritual of visually searching the horizon for any sign of marine traffic. I did that now, knowing full well that it would be fruitless. But I did it anyway, because hope never dies. You can't kill hope, no matter how ridiculously non-existent the possibilities.

I suddenly had another 'something' akin to a flashback. I remembered when I read "The Divine Comedy," by Dante, there was a passage seen by Dante and Virgil when they were entering the gates of Hates. The message was emblazoned on the frieze above the entrance; a warning, "ABANDON ALL HOPE YE WHO ENTER." Easy to say. Not easy to do!

So, I stood there, like a fool, gazing out at the flawless horizon. A clear blue ocean before me. The waves rolling in like a gentle monster, in search of the beach. There were many sea birds frolicking on the sand. They were hunting something; I knew not what it might be. But when I turned back toward what I had now dubbed "Charley Town," I encountered a surprise.

I almost missed seeing the creature, despite its huge size, because it moved in slow motion, like a sloth. It was the strangest looking whatever I had ever seen! It looked to be a combination of a coconut and a crab, and it weighed at least ten pounds! It clung to the bole of a coconut tree, about six feet off the ground. And as I looked around, I saw that there were dozens of them. Where had they come from? And the most important question of all was; were they good to eat?

There was one way to find out. I carefully pulled one from the bore of a coconut tree, and carried him with both hands to my campfire where I tossed him in. It seemed very inhumane, but I wasn't sure how to mercifully kill the thing without risking being badly pinched by its huge claws. However, the coals in the fire dispatched it quickly. I let it cook on one side for a minute, then used my bamboo pole to flip it over. Within ten minutes, I was raking it out of the coals onto fresh banana leaves. Now to get into it. I began with the monstrous claws.

I managed to break one off with the help of my broad-blade saber. I then managed to crack it open and tentatively took a bite of the steaming meat. I thought I would pass out from the delicious taste! The next thirty minutes were consumed with getting into my bonanza and eating every succulent tidbit! Then, I went to the nearest crab bearing coconut tree and grabbed another one! I repeated my previous actions and was rewarded with the same results. I was not just eating for the sake of survival. I was dining on meat that would be sold at a high price in the finest New Orleans restaurant!

I even softly blew on a small bite, cooling it and offered it to Phil. He accepted it. Ha! Now I was sharing the same food with my pet that I was eating. I didn't know why that was significant, but it was. I was slowly mastering this strange place that I had been tossed into. Each accomplishment was a triumph, a rush, another merit badge. Given time, I would be master of this realm!

I piled wood on my fire to build the flames high. Dark was approaching, and I wanted to push back the night, show it that I was here, and I would not cow-tow to the challenges that had been forced upon me.

The answers of how I came here, and why, would come, sooner or later. The question now was, how did I want to appear when they revealed themselves, and I faced them? Like a loser, or a winner? Would a cork pop to the surface when you released it from under water? Yes, certainly. Charley Flynt was like that cork! Nothing was going to defeat me! I am a winner. Winners never quit; quitters never win. I fished around in the pocket of my trousers and found the champagne cork. It had just this minute become a symbol. I needed to find some place to display it properly. It would be my daily reminder. I made a lanyard for it from some reeds and hung it around my neck. Nobody but me would know what it meant. But that didn't matter. Nobody else was here. So I needn't worry about looking like a fool.

I had mastered my environment to the point that I had established a routine, as such. And that routine, in the evening, included a bath in the lagoon before bed. And so, I did that, by the light of my very bright bonfire. Suddenly, I felt a tickling on my back. Then it spread to my sides and front. I could see well enough by the light of the fire and moon. At first, it scared the hell out of me. But then I began to see tiny fish who were pecking at small particles on my skin, including where I was peeling from being sun burned. Once I got past the surprise, it started to feel good. So, I stayed a bit longer in the water and let the little buggers clean me. It felt almost as good as a massage.

Filled with crab meat, washed and dappled, I made my way to the parrot perch and moved Phil to his inside quarters. Then I carefully laid down on my banana leaf covered cot and fell gently to sleep. As I dozed, I thought, tomorrow, I would make a second trip up the mountainside and further explore the cave. Some 'thing' deep inside me told me I needed to do that. The exploration of the cave was unfinished.

"It's hopeless, Charley. Regardless of where you and I start out, we wind up in the same place… at a dead end!"

I came up off of my cot at a start and uttered an oath. The voice was so close, so real, so … alive! And so intense! I was panting and in a cold sweat. If my memory was returning, I wished that it would just do it all at once, instead of torturing me like this with snippets.

Who was that woman? I recognized the voice but could not put a face to it. Damn blast it anyway! My frustration level was growing. Up until now, I had tried to keep it pushed down, where I didn't have to deal with it. But that was getting harder to do. I was beginning to suspect that 'how' I got here was somehow connected to a who. But which who? I couldn't remember one single face or name of anybody that I knew before coming here. Why?

Those questions caused another sleepless night. At break of dawn, I walked out to the beach. Maybe here, in the half light, I could spot distant lights on some ship. But a visual search of the horizon again verified there was nothing. Just a lot more of those strange looking, monstrous crabs, climbing up the coconut trees. Why had they started showing up? Was it mating season or something? I didn't really care what the reason was. All I did know was, they were very delicious to eat, and eating them had not affected my digestive system adversely.

On the other hand, they might disappear just as quickly as they had appeared. I had to be prepared for that. Enjoy them while they were here. Eat my fill. It's not like I had a refrigerator or a freezer to store anything. I headed back to Charley Town. I needed to get ready to take a second trip up the side of the mountain.

My second safari up the side of the mountain was as mystical as the first. The beauty of this place was hypnotic, stunning, indescribable, almost as if a master painter had painted a giant canvas. And then I thought, maybe one did! This place was too beautiful, too impeccable to be real. Yet, here it was! I could see it, touch it, feel it, smell it. I could bathe in its aura.

I started to notice more things this time, including the myriad of orchids in every color imaginable. They festooned the limbs and branches of trees, large or small. Some of the orchids emitted a delicate perfume, which I could detect when I sniffed deeply.

It didn't take that long to reach the cave, now that I knew it was there. The breeze was blowing from a slightly different direction today, so the way it hit the mouth of the cave made a soft moaning sound. It felt like the mountainside was talking to me.

I carefully negotiated my way along the narrow goat path to the cave. I entered and saw the old skeleton, still lying there in the same place where it had lain for the past hundred years, or maybe longer. I wasn't sure what I expected to find here. But my previous trip, as rich as it had been in treasures, seemed unfinished, somehow.

I looked around carefully. There didn't seem to be any other reason to hang around. I decided to sit on a small boulder which was positioned less than six feet away from the skeleton, and rest for a minute before starting my trip back down the mountain. But when I sat, something poked me against the back side of my upper thigh. I yelled 'Ouch!' and jumped up, then turned to see what had gaffed me. It appeared to be a short protrusion of some kind, sticking out from the boulder. I rubbed it with my fingers. This wasn't made of stone. It was metal! Then I used my knuckles to bang on the boulder. It made a metallic, hollow sound. This wasn't a rock at all! It was a 'what the hell,' happy surprise.

I got goosebumps. The piece of metal was apparently a leg of some kind. I grabbed it and struggled to pull it toward me. Whatever it was had been lying there for decades, so it was partially buried in the sandy dirt floor. But because the cave floor was mostly sand, it broke free without too much of a struggle. I slowly turned it over. It was a large, cast-iron cooking pot. A cooking pot! A bit rusty, but still in pretty good shape. I whooped with joy!

The question, was it in good enough shape to bother with? It had been here in this cave for a long, long time. Why was it not rusted to pieces? It was very heavy, thick cast-iron. Did the old timers use some kind of alloy when they made these things which resisted rust and prolonged the pot's life? Maybe so! Evidence before me would suggest they did.

Now! The challenge was, I guessed the old pot to weigh close to a hundred pounds, at least. How in the world did the owner of the broken legged skeleton ever manage to get that thing up the side of the mountain, then along that goat trail in front of this cave to get it here? He must have been as strong as a bull. But why here? Why lug it in here? He would have to fetch water to fill it and do something about a fire to cook in it. Lugging water along that goat trail would have been dangerous. I began to suspect that the old skeleton wasn't the sharpest knife in the drawer. No wonder he wound up breaking his leg!

Anyway, it was still somewhat of a mystery as to why he would choose this cave as his stronghold. Weird. What possible circumstances brought him here? Some mysteries are locked away in time and will never be solved. But that made it no less interesting to wonder about.

Well, no use worrying about it now. What I needed to do was make a decision about salvaging it. Would it be of enough use to me to lug back down the mountainside? The answer was, hell yes!

I decided to roll it to the mouth of the cave, then push it out. If it rolled all the way down to the stream, perhaps I could float it home. At least, most of the way.

I rolled my new treasure to the mouth of the cave. Not very hard to do. I looked down, toward the stream. It looked to be close to a hundred feet; about fifty feet straight down, then another fifty feet of slope, down to the water's edge. This old pot was made of cast-iron. If it slammed against any rocks on the trip down to the stream, it would crack like an eggshell and be worthless. But there was no choice. I was not going to risk carrying it along that goat trail and wind up like the skeleton, with a broken leg, or worse. I took a deep breath and pushed.

Predictably, the pot rolled like a ball downward, through the brush, making all kinds of racket as it snapped branches and hit things that made it gong like a bell. As it approached the stream, the area leveled off, and the brush was thick enough that it slowed the old pot down. It came to rest right at the edge of the stream. Success! I couldn't believe my good fortune!

I made my way back down the goat trail to the stream, then waded upstream a few yards to claim my new prize. So, the first leg of my experiment had gone well. How would leg number two go? As well? I sure hoped so.

I rolled the pot into the water, open top up. Although it sank down into the water about two thirds of the way because of its weight; still, it floated! All I had to do now was walk with it, guiding it along.

Sometime later, I arrived at the small waterfall just above the lagoon. I encountered a problem here, because the waterfall was filled with exposed rocks. If I pushed the pot over at this point, it would break for sure. So, I had no choice but to wrestle the pot down the incline beside the waterfall. It wasn't easy, and it was slow going. But what the hell else did I have to do? An hour later, I gazed at my new prize, sitting adjacent to my cookfire. I wasn't sure what I was going to do with it, yet. But I had managed to get it from the cave to Charley Town. Good for me!

This represented not only another usable tool, but another triumph! Slowly, but surely, Charley!

CHAPTER SIX

Memories

Staring at the pot, it occurred to me that the feel of warm water for a bath would be unbelievably wonderful. And so, I spent the next half hour filling the pot with water from the lagoon, using a seed pod husk from a palm tree as a large ladle. I guessed that the old pot would hold close to twenty gallons. It was black, and a little brown where rust had managed to get a bite on it. There were two islets, one on either side at the rim where I guessed that a wire handle had been at one time. That handle was long gone. But to me, it looked like it was brand new, from Worldmart!

I stacked branches around the pot and raked some coals from the main fire, over to the wood around the pot, to get it started. No big trick to accomplish. The water warming fire was blazing in no time. Lord, what I would give for a bar of soap! My reflection in the lagoon also told me that a comb would be nice. I hadn't combed my hair since my arrival here, and I was starting to look like an ad for a leaf blower. "One hundred MPH power guaranteed! The best blow-job you'll get this year!"

It took the better part of an hour, but at last, my warm bath was ready. I used a coconut shell for a scoop and reveled in pouring warm water over the top of my head, as I stood naked atop a pallet of fresh banana leaves. The feeling was hypnotic and took me away to a very deep mood. After bathing, I sat naked upon the banana leaf pallet and stared into the fire. The feeling was hypnotic.

I felt like the haze was lifting. Images started appearing in my mind. A beautiful blond woman stood at a window. She was talking. "We can't keep doing this, Charley. Leroy is starting to get suspicious."

"Why? We're being careful," I said.

"Because I love you, and I can't stand him touching me anymore. I pull back. He gets this awful hurt look in his eyes."

"So, divorce the pissant."

"Why, Charley? So, you can marry me?"

I had no response. I didn't want to marry her. I didn't want to marry anybody. I knew I wasn't fit for marriage. There had been one marriage in my life, and I had fucked it up royally! There! Another memory was knocking at the door.

"It's simple. Are you happy with him?"

The woman bowed her head. "No. Not for a long time."

"So, divorce his ass and move on. Life's too short to be miserable."

The vision and memory began to fade. I noticed the water remaining in the pot was starting to steam. It gave me an idea.

I donned my pants, or what was left of them, then went looking among the palm trees for one of those monster crabs. It didn't take long to find one, clinging to a palm bole, about five feet above the ground. I pulled him loose, being very careful to not let any part of me get caught in those huge pinchers. They looked like they could do some serious damage if they locked down onto you. Thank goodness the creature was very slow moving.

This was a particularly large specimen. I returned to the fire and carefully lowered him into the boiling water. The reaction and death were very quick. I waited about ten minutes before I fished him out of the boiling water, onto some waiting banana leaves. Then he had to cool. Finally, my supper began. The very first bite of crab claw told me boiling was the way to go! It was delicious beyond words. Succulent! Scrumptious! And as large as the crab was, just the one filled me. But I took my time and extracted every little morsel from the shell.

Then, it hit me. I could use that large crab carapace as a bowl and use it for multiple purposes. It could hold food, be used as a large scoop to move water from the lagoon to the pot. Why hadn't I thought of that before now? I would start saving the carapace from every crab I ate!

I finally reached a point where I could ignore it no longer. That short snippet of memory from the past was not very pleasant. Not very pleasant at all. I wasn't proud of the aftermath of that tete-a-tete. In truth, the blond and I kept seeing each other. It was risky, because her old man was as crazy as a shit house rat. He was also blind as a bat, and wore glasses with lenses that looked like the bottom of coke bottles. Problem was, he was as big as a house. If he ever jumped me, I would look like that pile of broken sticks around my fire.

He actually walked into a bar, looking for me and Marilyn one night. He was so fucking blind that we managed to duck out a back door before he saw us. We thought it was exciting, and funny at the time. Now, I realize how insensitive and cruel I had been.

Then came the night that we thought he was out of town, working at some refinery or something. So, we met and got very smashed, then went to my house for the real party. I screwed her all night, non-stop. She always was dynamite in bed! And putting it mildly, there is nothing we didn't do!

When we had driven home from the bar, Marilyn followed me in her car, and pulled in the driveway behind me. I lived in a little hamlet on the coast, south of Houston, called San Leon. Ninety percent of the houses there are beach houses, which, by description, are houses which sit on elevated pilings at least ten feet above the ground. Some are a lot higher than that. My house was one of those kinds of houses and faced the beach. An adjunct of Galveston Bay, called Dickinson Bay, was practically in my front yard.

The next morning, I woke up and made coffee. Then I wanted a cigarette and discovered that I was out. I pulled on my pants and shirt, then yelled to Marilyn in the bedroom, "Going to the store. Back in a minute." I didn't even have shoes on. Nobody would care. This was San Leon!

But when I started down the stairs, I saw that her car was behind mine. I turned around and went back into the house. I was going to ask her for her keys so I could move her car. But the store was only two blocks away. So, I just said fuck it, dug her keys out of her purse and drove her car the two short blocks to the convenience store.

What I didn't know was that her asshole husband, 'Leroy,' had doubled back from his job and had been watching my house from his pickup truck, a block away. As blind as the bastard was, when I got in Marilyn's car and pulled out of the driveway, all he saw was his wife's car. Seeing that, he assumed, logically, that his wife was leaving to go home. After her car went around the corner, Leroy started his pickup and drove to where Marilyn had been parked, behind my car, in my driveway!

He got out of his truck, carrying a huge twelve-gauge, double barreled shotgun, loaded with buckshot. He crept up the stairs, entered the unlocked front door and made his way in the half-light to the bedroom. Seeing the form beneath the sheets, and assuming it was me, he leveled the shotgun and yelled, "Hey, motherfucker! Wake up! I want you to see this coming!"

Still asleep, but hearing her husband's voice, Marilyn immediately raised up. Only problem was, her head was covered with the sheet. She apparently reached up to pull the sheet off so she could see, but it was too late.

Leroy didn't wait to confirm his target. He squeezed both triggers and unloaded that double barreled shotgun right into the chest of his wife. She screamed, momentarily, at the impact, which knocked her clear off of the bed, onto the floor.

Hearing the scream, Leroy dropped the gun, scrambled across the bed to the opposite side, screaming, "Marilyn! Marilyn! Marilyn?"

He pulled back the sheet and found his wife, dead, her lifeless eyes wide open. The shock was too much for him. Even though Marilyn was a cheating old bar fly, Leroy doted on her. He back tracked across the bed, picked up the shotgun, reloaded it and stuck the end of the barrel in his mouth. A moment later, Leroy suffered no more anguish, or anything else. His brains were all over my ceiling and bedroom wall.

I had gotten into a conversation with the clerk at the convenience store which lasted about ten minutes. By the time I returned home from the store, car loads of cops were showing up at my house, red and blue lights flashing all over the place. I saw them as I turned the corner onto my street and wondered what the hell was going on. That is, until I saw Leroy's truck in my driveway. It didn't take a member of Mensa to figure out the scenario.

The cops weren't going to let me into my own house. But then they needed somebody to identify the bodies. As I walked back down the steps, shaken, in shock, and weak, I overheard two cops talking to each other. Cop 1: "Sumbitch blew his own wife away!"

Cop 2: Pointing at me. "Wasn't his wife he was after. He was trying to take out that asshole, over there!"

The cop was right. When Leroy saw Marilyn's car drive away, that was what he had been waiting for. I was his target, and he missed. That could have been me they were loading onto a gurney and covering up with a blanket.

Something happened to me that day. Something deep and earth shaking. I felt a combination of fear and anger. Most of all, I felt sick.

There was a deep hatred inside of me. But I wasn't sure who the hatred was aimed at. Was it for me? For life? For Leroy? And then I felt 'it'!

Something happened inside of me that defies any description. It was like some entity entered my body. I didn't understand what was happening, but I had never been so frightened. There was suddenly a part of my own being that I was no longer in control of. But what was it?

No more memories, please! Not for the present. That one little sojourn into the past was enough of a trip down memory lane for now. I just wanted to sleep and forget what I had just remembered. I feared that would be impossible. You can't 'un-ring' a bell!

I moved Phil from his outside perch to the one inside the hut and crashed. Not that it did much good. I lay awake for hours, listening to the tree frogs, and other night sounds, and thinking. Although 'thinking' was the last frapping thing I wanted to do! One of the things I was thinking about was, out of all the fucking dreams in the world, why was that one the first one to come to the surface, like a floating mine? You'd think that memories would have some order to them as far as priority goes. But then, maybe not! Maybe they're like dreams and make no sense at all.

A few days ago, I yearned to remember 'something,' 'anything.' Now, I was frightened of what memories would come. I was divided. One part of me wanted to remember the past. The bigger half of me did not. But I knew without a doubt, now that it had started, memories would come, welcome or not. There simply was no way to stop them. The question was, what would I discover? What other nightmares would surface about 'Good ol' Charley?'

Dawn found me standing on the beach, looking out at the clear blue sea. It was deceptively tranquil. A clear, uninterrupted surface with waves slowly rolling in. But I knew that just beneath that surface, death was a daily part of life. It was routine that the bigger fish ate the smaller ones. Big fish *always* ate the smaller fish, even on land!

On the beach, small fiddler crabs scurried about on the sand, chasing the water's edge as it receded, then ran up the beach when a wave rolled in. For some reason, the sea birds, feeding on micro-organisms in the wet sand, ignored the small crabs.

It was very easy to be seduced by this, to feel a part of it. Why? I was not from here. I was from a different part of the world. Maybe it was because everything here seemed to accept me, not question who I was, or what I was. Nothing here judged me! Not being judged. Wow! What a feeling!

Carlos (Charles) Flynt: Born to a Mexican mother, and an American father in Tampico, Mexico. My father was a drunk who, thankfully, worked on gulf shrimp boats and was on the water a couple of months at a time. It was when he came home from those trips that hell would kick into gear.

I remember him beating my mother. I also remember him making me drink beer and telling me it was my mother's breast milk. I got dizzy, sick and then threw up all over the floor. My dad laughed.

I must have been almost five by the time my mother left him. She took advantage of one of his thirty-day sea jaunts to pack up and split. She brought me to the Texas border and left me in the care of the state of Texas. The last time I ever saw her was in the courthouse in Brownsville, Texas. I was sitting in a big, dark wood chair with a slatted back.

My mother kissed me, looked at me and said, "Nunca tenga miedo!" (Never be afraid.) Then, she was gone. Walked away. The very last image I have of her is her back, and the sound of her heels, as she walked on that tile floor. I'll never forget the awful, echoing acoustics in that fucking courthouse. It made my crying sound all the louder.

I could not understand why my mother had abandoned me. I did not learn until many years later, her actions were driven by the fact that she was dying of TB. She did not want to leave me with her parents in Guadalajara. They were old and could have never wrangled a five year old sprout. But she did want me to be able to take advantage of my American birth right. Since my father was an American, I had dual citizenship until the age of twenty-one, at which time I would have to make a choice, Mexican, or American. That is, unless that choice was made for me by adoptive parents.

After being farmed out to several families, many times, and being rejected 'many times,' mostly because I spoke no English, I was finally adopted by a family who were religious zealots.

The family that adopted me spoke no Spanish, and I spoke no English, except for a very muddy sounding "merie criestmos!" Their motive in adopting me was, they had lost a son at age nine. When they saw me, they were convinced that I was the reincarnation of that son. By the time they figured out that wasn't the case, that I was just a little half breed Mexican, looking for a fresh tortilla, the shock was too much. That's when the abuse started, and got progressively worse, particularly where 'she' was concerned. My adopted dad seemed to care about me, and spent time with me, when he could. But when he wasn't home, 'home' was the belly of the beast.

School was no better. In those days, there were separate water fountains for "Mexicans" as well as separate restrooms. I couldn't use the Mexican's water fountain because I looked like a Gringo, and I had a Gringo's name. I couldn't use the white kid's fountain because I spoke no English. I sounded like a "Meskin, a bean burner, a pachuco." The same applied for restrooms. I wound up drinking out of the water hose, which tasted awful, because in those days, hoses were made of rubber. I had to walk across the street from the schoolhouse, where there was a field covered with tall weeds, so I could pee.

I took this crap for a couple of years. Then a bunch of white kids, led by a freckle-faced bully named Billy, caught me drinking from the white kid's fountain and started to push me around. Something inside me snapped and I laid into about four of them, knocking every one of them down. Then I singled out Billy and beat the living hell out of him. I hit him. He hit the ground and started yelling like the pussy he was. I landed on top of him and began whaling on him. I hit him so many times that my arms got tired, and his face looked like an over inflated balloon. After that day, nobody gave me any shit. I drank and peed anywhere I wanted. Not only that, within a few days, I had a couple of toadies.

I learned from that. And what I learned from that experience was that nothing is ever given to you out of the goodness of somebody's heart. If you want something, you have to take it. There endeth the lesson, tall grass and short!

CHAPTER SEVEN

It's All Coming Back Now

I was crestfallen. Remembering was a double-edged sword.
I turned and walked away from the beach, back toward Charley Town. Phil would be wanting his breakfast, and to be moved from the perch in the hut to his outside 'lanai', where there was more danger, but a better view. It occurred to me that to improve safety for my little bird, I needed to build an overhang, coming off the front of the hut for at least eight or ten feet. That would be my next project. If Phil was protected beneath a cover, raptors would be far less likely to see him and attack. By now, I loved my little Phil. I didn't want anything to happen to him. I would build the overhang right away.

For now, I would pick bananas and a mango or two along the way back to Charley Town, so that I could share with Phil. His parents were also still flying in with regurgitated 'pre-digested' food for him. So, Phil was in pretty good shape. The parents didn't want to hang around for long, but while they visited, there seemed to be an acceptance of me. Why not? I had saved their baby!

And what about my breakfast? Christ, what I would give for a hot, steaming cup of coffee! I envisioned three eggs, sunnyside up, parked next to a ration of hash browns. Maybe a couple of strips of bacon, maybe a big, buttery biscuit to round it all out. Damn-damn-damn!

Back at Charley Town, I peeled a beautiful mango and cut up pieces to put in Phil's cup, along with some pieces of banana. Then I changed his water. As I fussed over him, I said, "Good morning, Phil. How you making it this morning?"

Suddenly, the little bird said, "Good morning, Phil!" My eyes grew wide with wonder. I was smiling. It had only been a few days! How had that little rascal learned to talk so quickly? I laughed out loud. I was taking tremendous pride and delight in this simple moment. It felt wonderful!

Well, that certainly made my day! Ha Ha! Ho Ho! Phil and I would learn to say many things together! Finally! Something to laugh about in this place where, up until now, there had only been puzzlement.

The next thing I would teach Phil to say is, "Thank you, Phil!" I said it to him a couple of times before I turned my attention to other things. He listened intently, cocking his head to one side and looking at me. I smiled again at this simple pleasure.

Several days ago, I had fashioned a fish trap and sank it in the lagoon, near the delta. I decided to check on it and see if I had any luck.

As I walked toward the delta, I stepped on a sea-shell. It activated a memory, instantly, as if the past was happening in real time.

When I was around eight, I had a BB gun. Everything was a target. For some reason, there was a soda pop bottle lying in the grass in the back yard. I shot at it and broke it with the BB gun. Then, like all kids, I forgot about it. Did I pick up the broken pieces of the bottle? No, of course not. That would have been too logical for an eight-year-old.

But I found those pieces a few days later when, chasing my puppy around the back yard! I stepped on the broken glass and cut my left foot all the way to the bone. Luckily, my dad was home. He applied a tourniquet around my leg, and we made an emergency run to the doctor. I got sewed up. But that was not the end of it.

A few days later, I was awakened by my adopted mother, who was tying me, spread eagle to the four corners of my bed. My father had gone to work, and my mother was foaming at the mouth.

"You little bastard! I told you to not shoot at anything that could break, with that damned BB gun. You cost us a big doctor bill with that stupid stunt of yours!"

That's all she said. I was terrified. I didn't know what she was going to do. But I soon found out. Once I was tied so that I could not move or escape. She took my BB gun, went into the kitchen and emptied the BBs into a frying pan. She heated them red hot, then brought the frying pan into the bedroom to where I was tied and poured them over my naked top. I screamed bloody and continued to scream. The heated BBs rolled off of me, onto the bed, where they rolled up against me and became wedged between me and the sheet. I passed out from the pain and woke up in the hospital. There were no state agencies in those days designed to protect children from this kind of thing, or anything else for that matter. It all came under the heading of 'discipline.' Children were considered property and 'you just didn't interfere'.

Meanwhile, I spent close to a week in the hospital. My mother had claimed that I got too close to the stove while she was cooking, and she had spilled something hot on me. Did my father believe it? Most likely not. But in the fifties, divorce was not really an option. Mores were different. And I began to suspect the real cause of their first child's death was no 'accident'. The story was that he fell in the bathtub & hit his head. As a result, a tumor began to grow in his head which took over a year to kill him. But did he 'fall', or was he pushed, or slammed? The longer I stayed in the Flynt household, the more I was convinced of the latter.

For four years, I lived in that house in mortal fear, believing my adopted mother was a murderer. Then, when I was twelve years old, she confirmed my suspicions. In a fit of rage, she pointed a loaded shotgun at me and pulled the trigger. There was a sickening 'click' sound, but nothing happened. She muttered, "What the hell?" and pointed the gun toward the ceiling

She tried to open the breach and see if the gun was loaded. It was, but with an old shell. There had been a delay. The shotgun discharged, blowing a hole in the bedroom ceiling, right over the top of my head.

I bolted out the door and ran pell-mell down the street as fast as I could go. I didn't look back to see if she had come out of the house to follow me. She wouldn't do that. After all, she had a reputation to maintain with the neighbors!

Thus ended my childhood, at twelve years of age. I wandered around, confused for a day or so. There was a community college not too far from our house with lots of places to hide and especially at night. So, I hid there while I tried to figure things out. I knew I could never go back home. That was not a home anyway. That crazy bitch was over the top, nuts. I had known it for a long time. I just thought I could live with it. I never dreamed she would go this far. But why was I surprised?

There were many things she had done when she lost it. One time, at the golf course, I was watching some ducks swim in a small pond on the golf course. I finally got bored and went back to the club house. My parents were there, but my mother was red faced with fury. "Where have you been we've been waiting for you close to an hour."

"I'm sorry. I was watching some ducks over there in the pond."

"Ducks? We waited for you an hour while you were watching ducks? Get in the damned car, right this minute!

As we were driving on the private road between the club house and the main highway, she lost it. "Stop the car!" Dad stopped and she got out, found a stick, then opened the back door of the car, grabbed me by the arm and yanked me out of the back seat. Then she began beating me with the stick. The thing was, the stick was a branch from a mesquite tree. It had thorns and each time she hit me on the butt or back, she knocked holes in me. I went into shock and wound up in the hospital again.

I think she and Dad must have had some kind of row over that incident, because they didn't do much talking to each other for the next few days. And dad tried to get me out of the house as much as possible for a while. My mother cooled it, for a while. But it didn't take long for the 'show' to resume.

Eventually, as I hid in the community college and got hungrier, a plan began to emerge in my mind, and I hitch hiked my way to Brownsville. A nice old lady who owned a Mexican restaurant took me under her wing and fed me, plus let me sleep in her guest bedroom a few nights. But Brownsville was not my destination. Tampico, Mexico was. So, the old woman gave me bus fare, helped me get across the border and made sure I had survival money to hold me for at least a month. As the bus got ready to pull out of Matamoros, she assured me I would always have a home and a job if I decided to double back. She had been kind to me for no reason that I could understand, other than I was a kid. It felt very strange. I wasn't afraid for my life for the first time in a very long time.

The bus made its way out of Matamoros and headed south, toward Tampico, Mexico. Three hours later, as the bus entered the city limits of Tampico, it passed the Plaza De Toros Monumental, the bull ring. I started hollering "ALTO! STOP!" It was the one place I recognized from my childhood. My mother had brought me here, because she had been family friends with a bullfighter, and I got to see him fight in the ring. It was a pageant that I would never forget.

The custodian of the bullring had a house full of kids. He figured one more didn't matter, one way or the other. So he took me in. It was interesting how quickly my Spanish came back to me, even though the Flynt's had forbidden me to speak Spanish, or even speak English with a Spanish accent. "You must leave all of that behind you, Charles. You're in America now. We speak English in this country. *'Only'* English. It is our national language."

Several days after I was a guest in the home of Mr. De Alba, the custodian of the Plaza De Toros, a man arrived in a truck with seven bulls for the coming Sunday's bullfight. The driver was a man named Don Tiburcio. He was the owner of the ranch. He delivered the bulls personally because he was short of drivers. When he saw me, he pointed and asked, "Who is this little 'juedito' (blondie)?"

"He is a guest in my home," Mr. De Alba said. A run-away from some place in Texas. His mother tried to kill him, loca chinga!"

"Really? What is your name?"

"Charley. I mean, Carlos."

"Well, Carlos, would you like to come with me? I have a ranch. I will give you a job, and a home away from any kind of cruelty."

I didn't need to think about it for more than a second. "Yes, I would love that! Thank you, Don Tiburcio!"

It seemed very natural when I was offered a job on a ranch where fighting bulls were raised. I gladly accepted, and wound up living high in the mountains of Saltillo, on a ranch that seemed to spread-out forever. This ranch was not limited to livestock. It was also a 'finca' (farm) and was very diversified. Don Tiburcio had cotton fields, orange groves and a mango orchard.

I learned many things while living on that ranch, starting with how to ride a horse. We had no TV on the ranch. For entertainment, the vaqueros and campocinos would gather around a big campfire at night and commiserate, tell stories of the day while they hand rolled cigarettes to smoke and sipped from their bottles of agua ardiente, a home-made version of moonshine.

Many problems, imaginary and otherwise were deliberated and often solved around that campfire. All possible considerations were discussed at one time or another. Opinions were espoused, listened to and respected. If only the world could listen in, they would have offered solutions to almost everything from marriage, to child rearing, to commerce and politics! There would be no wars, no poverty, no strife of any kind. Especially between man and women.

Cowboy philosophy! When I got older, I realized there was more wisdom shared around that campfire than I had thought at the time. Now, as I stared into my own campfire in the evenings, it made those memories easier to recall. And those memories gave me something to smile about. Something to ease the loneliness. As I began to get drowsy, I remembered that my nickname among those cowboys had been "Flaco." The Spanish word for skinny.

I waded into the delta and retrieved my fish trap. It had been shattered by something. Apparently, a big fish had gotten trapped in it, but was strong enough to get out! At least it showed me there were fish to be caught. I just needed to make a stronger trap.

I peeled strips of bamboo and started all over again, making sure this time to carefully weave everything together tightly, strongly, and then tie everything together firmly. At last, the new and improved trap was ready. From end to end, it was almost four feet long and eighteen inches in diameter. I placed a heavy stone in it and took it to the delta to try again.

CHAPTER EIGHT

A Litany of Memories

When I reached the age of 20, it came time to leave the ranch, and, for that matter, leave Mexico. I returned to the United States, although I didn't have a clue what I was going to do to make a living. Don Tiburcio had treated me like a son and made sure that I got a formal education so I wouldn't wind up having to ride a horse all of my life. But what now?

I had a degree from The University of Technology in Monterrey. But truth told, that had been mostly wasted time. I didn't really learn anything useful. What I did do was learn how to bang the dean's daughter, who worked as a secretary at the university. To show her appreciation, she doctored my attendance records and grades. The dean was on to the fact that I was doing 'something' to the paperwork, but damned if he could figure out what, or how.

He called me into his office on one occasion, and pointed at an attendance sheet, saying accusingly, "Look! It says right here that you were in class on September the seventeenth, and I happen to know for a fact that you were in Mexico City the day before, for some reason or other."

"So? I flew back," I lied. He couldn't prove otherwise, so in total frustration, he kicked me out of his office.

Still, having that diploma to hang on my wall did nothing to help me with the problem at hand. How was I going to make a living? Ranching is all I knew how to do. But making a good living in Mexico either required special skills, or family money. I had neither. So, I returned to the United States, and because I had been interviewed by a television station in Laredo once upon a time, I stopped in to visit the manager. I thought maybe he could give me some advice. He did that and much more. He gave me a job, in advertising sales! I was fascinated.

To train me, he put me on the street with a guy named Danny, who was a singer on the side and had an ego the size of a watermelon truck. And Danny wanted to treat me like I just got off of one. One day we were in the office, sitting across from each another at a table, making phone calls. I picked up the phone and started to dial a number, but Danny didn't like the way I was dialing. "You don't have to dial the whole prefix here in Laredo, just the three," and he pushed the button down, disconnecting my call. That was it. I got up and hit Danny across the side of the head with the heavy receiver, knocking him out of his chair, onto the floor. He was out like a light.

Amazingly, I did not get fired for doing that, because as it turned out, nobody in the whole station liked Danny. Silently, I was cheered, but I was also moved from the TV station to the radio station, where they needed a salesperson very badly. They made me sales manager, and I found reasonable success there. I say reasonable because in those days, there wasn't a lot of money in Laredo. The potential for making any real money simply did not exist. So, I did the best I could, and compensated myself the best way that I could in other ways.

One of those ways was to accept the position of weatherman at the TV station for added income. The station manager's wife had been doing it but was tired of it. She had other interests. Only thing was, I was not a meteorologist, so I needed to be trained. And the only person to train me was the station manager's wife. She did that and I became a pretty good weatherman. I did crazy stuff like go on camera in the middle of the summer, when it hadn't rained in months, wearing a slicker. I would do the entire broadcast without ever making a single reference to the slicker. Everything was peachy until the station manager figured out that his wife and I were conducting what might be described as, 'extra-curricular classes in continuing education.'

Well, it was great while it lasted. After my dismissal from the TV -and- the radio station, I moved to Corpus Christi, where I went to work for a rock and roll A M radio station. I had the advertising bug now. I found out that I was good at it. Not only sales but writing. I wrote all of the commercials for my clientele. I would write a 'spec spot,' get one of the station jocks to record it, then take a portable tape recorder to the customer and play it for them. Nine times out of ten, they bought my idea and signed an advertising contract. I was having a ball. I was a reasonably sized big frog in a semi small pond!

By now, the Flynts were both deceased. They were buried side by side in a local cemetery. I found out where, then went to visit the gravesite. I had a strange feeling as I stood there, looking down at the graves. I don't know how long I stood and stared, but before leaving, I unzipped and watered my adopted mother's grave. That was my solitary visit. I never went back again.

Then, my life changed forever. I met Grady. And when I did, I felt myself entering another era, another phase of my life. There is a mystery about romantic attraction which is called, "chemistry." It is very real, although nobody understands exactly how it works. Two of the most unlikely matches in the world can meet, and WHAM! Love happens. That is how it was between me and Grady.

The earth moved beneath my feet like an earthquake. She took my breath away. I had never known anything like this before. It was entirely new to me, and very frightening. Frightening because for the first time in my life, I didn't feel like I was in control. I was vulnerable. It was wonderful and frightening at the same time.

I was obsessed. All I could think about day and night was Grady. When I wasn't with her, I wanted to be. And when I was with her, I was at a loss for words. I worshipped her. I worshipped the ground she walked on. What do you say to a woman who is a goddess in your eyes, who you are in awe of, who stuns you, merely to look at? I could not have been more mesmerized if I had been in the presence of Mona Lisa. And maybe that was a big part of the problem. She wasn't just a woman to me. She was holy.

Grady was five feet two inches tall, auburn hair that she cropped just above her shoulders. She had dark brown eyes, a perfect build and she had a smile that made her look like a shy model. Although she lived in Corpus Christi, she was born in Laredo, had Spanish ancestry (from Spain) and her last name was Almendarez. From the moment I met her, my mission was to change that last name to Flynt.

As it turned out, that wasn't too hard to do. Grady was a virgin when I met her, something I set about changing with all due dispatch. Not because it was some kind of a macho challenge. But because I wanted to touch what no one else had ever touched, to be a part of the holy grail. I had to possess Grady, to make her mine. She was the impossible dream. And yet, here she was, right in front of me with that lilting laugh and those incredibly beautiful dark eyes.

I was so obsessed with Grady and being one with her that I wasn't very careful, plus she was inexperienced, and wound up pregnant. Grady was beside herself. She was bouncing off the walls. She was a good, a pure woman. This kind of thing was unheard of in her moral belief system.

I guess she was frightened that I would kiss her goodbye and tell her to have a good life. I couldn't do that. It never entered my mind. I was deeply in love for the first time in my life, and I wanted to do the right thing. I asked her to marry me. She didn't really want to get married, but now she needed a name for this unborn child. Her sense of decency demanded it. And so, we had a small, private ceremony in my apartment with only a couple of friends present as witnesses. She became Mrs. Charley Flynt.

For our honeymoon, I suggested a road trip down through Mexico, along the east coast, to Tampico, and then beyond, all the way to the Yucatan Peninsula, to visit several Mayan archaeological sites. In hindsight, that may not have been the best choice. The road was long and hot and arduous. Although our car was air conditioned, the long road day after day wore Grady out. We should have just taken a flight; two hours to the Mexican Riviera, or Cancun. From there, we could have rented a car. The ancient Mayan city of Chichen Itza was only a one hour drive from the coast. But, that is not what we did. I think that is when my guilt started.

In the Yucatan, one thing happened which made everything else on the trip shrink to insignificance. Following a very hot day visiting one of the Mayan archaeological sites and climbing pyramids, Grady was taking a nap in our hotel room. I was in the hotel bar, yakking with some other tourists, drinking a couple of beers, and talking about the Maya Indians.

An old woman, dressed in black, sitting at a table across the room from the bar, kept staring directly at me, unblinking. After a while, her eyes began to bore into me. It was unnerving, so I excused myself, left my stool at the bar, and walked over to her table. I sat down across from the old hag and confronted her.

Translated from Spanish: "You've been staring at me for the last hour," I said. "Is something on your mind?"

Unruffled, the old hag said, "You and your wife are expecting a child. The child will be a male child. He will grow up to hate you and become your sworn enemy. Nothing you can do will change this destiny. Beware. That is all I have to tell you. Heed the warning."

Then, the old hag rose and walked out of the bar, using a cane for support. I sat frozen in my chair. What the hell kind of crazy horse shit was that, which I had just encountered? Crazy or not, I never forgot that moment, or the old hag's words. And it was the first time I had ever encountered someone who might have been from the spirit world, which I felt then, and still feel, was the case.

And here is what reinforced that belief: I got up from the table, stunned, and went back to the bar. After climbing back on a barstool and getting a fresh drink... a strong one! I looked across at the bartender, pointed at the table and said, "Do you know that old bruja that was just sitting at that table over there?"

The bartender looked quizzically at me, then at the table where I was pointing. "Bruja, Señor?"

"Yeah, yeah, the old broad dressed in black that just left. You know her?"

The bartender looked puzzled.

"Did you not see an old woman sitting across from me at that table over there?"

"I only saw you, sitting alone, and I wondered why," the bartender replied.

I never told Grady about the encounter. It would have shaken her. But I also never forgot it, for the old hag's premonition turned out to be true.

I sat by my campfire that night, staring into the flames. This thing with memories coming back to me was a double-edged sword. There were a lot of things that I was remembering that I didn't particularly want to remember. They served no purpose except to bedevil me. It was like having my face held down in a toilet, and a voice saying, "Look at this, you sonofabitch! Look what you did!"

There was a part of me that had not been a very nice person. That Charley would have cooked Phil instead of bringing him fresh fruit and trying to teach him how to talk. I felt that I was no longer the narcissistic Charley. That one was dead, thank God! But at what point did that transformation take place? That was the memory I wanted! Things were coming back to me in a flood. I felt reasonably sure, as much as I was remembering, that everything would be revealed to me; laid out on a table with a bright light so I would be compelled to examine everything closely, no matter how finite the detail. Upon realizing that, I felt apprehensive. Would I be able to handle whatever was behind the veil? Or would it crush me and leave me a sobbing mess? The more I remembered, the more apprehensive I became.

CHAPTER NINE

Love, Thou Art a Double-Edged Sword!

Grady and I had a fight. I don't remember what the fight was about, and to me, it was so minor that it wasn't worth all the fuss. I treated it like water off a duck's back. But Grady took it seriously and, she disappeared! As in, *really* disappeared. Not for a few days, but for several months. I have never known such agony. Not a minute went by that I didn't worry where she was, or how she was doing. She was, after all, carrying my child. Regardless of what that old bruja in Mexico had said, this was my child. Deep inside, I wanted to believe that the bruja was full of shit. What kind of an off-the-wall prediction was that anyway? She must have been drinking Ixtabentun!

Meanwhile, the pain of loss consumed me. Basically, it wrecked my life. I couldn't think of anything else. My sales began to suffer. I spent more time in bars, even during work hours. I was fired from my job. I needed to get a grip. And I did try to. But I was in hell, a living, burning hell, where each proceeding moment brought no relief. Only more agony to tear at my soul and make me wonder what the fuck I was living for. Time was not merciful. My pain didn't lessen with each passing day. It got worse. I found myself drowning in agony. I had to gasp for breath.

When one spends any time at all in bars, they learn quickly that bars are a separate world. They are infested by bar flies, whores and drunks.

In many cases, the drunks are the bar flies; old, burned-out, over the hill broads with raspy voices and sagging tits, sucking on cigarettes, who can be had for the price of a cold beer. But one day, a woman named Amy took pity on me at a vulnerable moment when I badly needed some pity. We drank together, got plowed together, and then went to my place together where we rolled around in the bed together.

Afterwards, I felt guilty because up until then, I had been completely faithful to Grady. The mere thought of touching someone else would have been repugnant to me. I had been faithful because she had been my world. But now she was gone. Just up and disappeared over what I felt was nothing. Therefore, my infidelity was justified. I wasn't perfect by any stretch of the imagination. But I loved Grady enough that I would have gladly listened to any reasonable complaint and attempted to reach an agreement. I hadn't been given that chance. Grady just disappeared. I came home from work one day to find her gone. She had packed a suitcase and left a couple of things lying on the bed. Things that I had bought for her that I thought meant something to her. There they were, lying on the bed like a slap in the face.

Obviously, I had immediately tried calling her workplace. They told me that she had taken a leave of absence. I called her sister and pled with her to tell me where Grady was, but all she would tell me is that Grady was alright. Then the bitch hung up.

Somewhere along the way, my pain and sorrow went through a metamorphosis and turned into anger. I simply did not deserve the punishment of missing Grady every moment of every day, hurting over her, crying over her every day, worrying about her every day. I started spending more time in bars, and fucked everything I could find. The nastier the dirty-legged whore, the better! After all, I wasn't attempting to 'make love.' All I wanted to do was punish myself, disgrace myself. Disgust myself!

Then, I reached the phase of trying to form 'meaningful' relationships, but that was out of the question. Relationships still weren't what I wanted. What I wanted was to outrun the incessant, gut-wrenching pain. The torment that tortured me twenty-four hours a day. I turned into a very angry, bitter person. The world had fucked me around, and I wanted revenge.

One Saturday, my anger reached a boiling point. I pulled my old .357 out of the closet, loaded it and went to Grady's sister's house. I didn't knock on the door, I just opened it and walked in. I found her in the kitchen, preparing supper. A boyfriend was sitting on a stool at the cook island sipping on a glass of wine, chatting. I stopped directly in front of Marcie, the sister.

"You've got to tell me where Grady is," I said.

She looked up at me with uncaring, contemptable eyes. "I can't do that."

"Yes, you can. And before I leave here, you will."

The boyfriend got up and started to walk around the cook island. He looked at me with his best attempt at intimidation. "You'd better get out of here, or..."

I was wearing a loose-fitting Hawaiian shirt, which easily concealed the .357 tucked into my belt. Now, I reached under my shirt and pulled out the gun. I pressed the end of the barrel against the boyfriend's forehead.

"There ain't no 'or'," I said very calmly. "You stand very still, right where you are, Hop-along, or your brains are going to be all over the taco meat."

Marcie's eyes lost their insolent gaze and were now the size of saucers. "All I want to know is, where's Grady, so that I can go to her and try to work out our problem, whatever that problem is. Now, you are going to tell me, or in about half a minute, you're going to be cooking for one."

Marcie bowed her head and took a deep breath. "She's in California. L A, living with one of our cousins."

"I need the address."

"It's in my address book. I'll write it down."

"Good. You do that. And focus on the problem at hand. Don't get any ideas about being a hero and quietly calling the cops, or people are going to start dying. You're looking at a desperate man who doesn't much give a fuck whether he lives or dies. You hear me talking?"

Marcie had tears running down her cheeks. She tried to wipe them away with her hand as she nodded yes.

"I'm going to take those tears as a sign that you understand. Now, go get that address."

Marcie went to an end table by her couch and opened a drawer where a small journal was. She took it out, opened to the right page, then brought it back to the cook island. She grabbed a pad of sticky notes and a pen, then with a hand shaking badly , she wrote the address down. I took the piece of paper from her.

"Thank you. Now, both of you listen to me very carefully because I am going to give you important instructions that, if you and Hop-along here are wise, you will follow to the letter. I am going to leave. Your first instinct will be to pick up the phone and call the fuzz. I strongly recommend that you resist that temptation, and project into the future. If you call the cops, they will come arrest me and haul me away. But I will make bail, and when I do, I will circle back here and kill both of you. With luck, I'll catch you in bed, fucking, and get both of you with one shot. I hate wasting bullets. The cops will most likely arrest me again, but I don't care. Living without Grady is worse than any death I might face. So, you are going to do nothing and stay healthy. Next, you are going to want to call Grady and tell her what has happened here. Don't do that either, for the same reason. You could have helped me a long time ago and prevented me from reaching this point of desperation. But you didn't. You were cold hearted and didn't give a fuck about my pain. Translated, what that means is, I really want to kill you anyway, so it won't take much to push me over the edge. Sabe?"

Marcie nodded yes again, as tears coursed down her cheeks. I turned to the boyfriend, the barrel of my pistol was still pressed against his forehead. "You got it, Hop-along?" He mumbled 'Yes." The fear showed in his eyes.

"Good," I said. "You're smarter than you look. Now, what I am going to do is go to L A, find Grady and try to talk to her. If that talk does not result in a reconciliation, I will walk away and let her live her life. But I *am* going to have the chance to talk to her. Do you understand what I'm saying so far? Do you have any questions?"

Marcie shook her head no. I turned to the boyfriend. "What about you, Hop-along? You got it so far, or do I need to use smaller words?"

"I've got it," the boyfriend said.

"Good, because I really don't like having to explain shit twice."

I turned back to Marcie. "Let this little meeting be a lesson to you about the advantage of compassion and mercy. The quality of mercy is not strained. That would have prevented this."

I sniffed the air. "Better turn down that heat a little. Your taco meat is burning. Or maybe that's Hop-along here. His armpits are on fire. Now, in closing, I just want to say that your cooperation is as appreciated as it is wise. I repeat, you are looking at a desperate man. And if it makes you feel any better about your cooperation, just let me assure you that none of this was a bluff. I would have happily killed you both if anything would have gone wrong. Now, my question is, are you going to play it smart and just chill when I walk out that door? Or will you scramble for the phone?"

"We aren't going to do anything. I give you my word," the boy-friend said.

"Your word? Okay, good thinking, Hop-along. And by the way, you need to do something with that hair. That shit was over with in the seventies, along with disco and leisure suits. I'll be leaving you now. Have a nice day, and don't move a muscle, even to fart, for at least five minutes. Once more; do nothing, stay alive. Cross me, and I will make it my life's quest to put both of you in an early grave. Enjoy your tacos!"

I walked out of Marcie's house with the sticky note in my shirt pocket. Within hours, I was on a red-eye to L A.

She never saw it coming. Grady opened her apartment door, presumably en route to drop the baby off at day care and then go to work. I was standing there, at the door. I said very calmly, "Let's go back inside. We need to have a talk."

She turned as white as a sheet, then reversed direction to walk back into the apartment. Her cousin was there, sitting on the sofa. "Do you want me to call the police?" the cousin said.

"No," Grady said.

"That would be an extremely bad idea," I said to the cousin. "Why don't you just tootle along," I said to her, holding the door open. The cousin looked at me, then at Grady.

"That would probably be best," Grady confirmed. The cousin rose from the sofa, grabbed her purse and headed for the door, doing her best to give me a disparaging look as she passed me.

"Don't bother with that," I said, staring at her. "Use your energy to look for a new roommate."

The cousin went out the door, and I closed it behind her. I sat across from Grady and held my child for the first time. He looked so tiny, so innocent. I thought about the bruja's words and came to the conclusion that she was nuts. This was just a tiny baby boy, wanting to find his way in this world. How could anybody not love him? How could I not love him?

Two hours later, Grady was packing her stuff, and I was loading it into her car. We were going home to Texas. She left the cousin a note, and we locked the door on the way out. I have hated California ever since that day.

CHAPTER TEN

Turn the Page

Back home in Corpus Christi, I tried to restore some normalcy to our lives. I tried to be the person Grady wanted me to be. I worked hard at my new job, and quickly developed a growing client list. I started making good money. My life was getting back to normal, and I should have been pain-free.

But something was wrong! Something was different deep inside of me. Something had changed. Although the California episode was over and behind us, *it wasn't!* I felt a deep-seated resentment. There was an anger which it seemed I had no control over. It kept trying to bubble to the surface. I had been put through unbridled hell for what, as it turned out, was a minor problem that was talked through in a matter of minutes. I swallowed hard and kept it down for a long time. But like a cancer, it kept growing. It was a disease. But I didn't understand that for a long time. Way too long!

I felt like a fool. Never had I been so taken for granted in my life. And the person who was at the root of that was the woman I loved heart and soul. Why? It made no sense to me. How can you love somebody, and yet be so indifferent about hurting them? Didn't she realize what she was doing to me in those six months?

I found myself stopping at one bar or another on the way home and drinking a few beers, when I should have been home, bouncing my baby on my knee. Eventually, a few beers became several. I constantly told myself to let it go. It was over. I got my life back, now quit sniveling about it and move on. The reason a rear-view mirror is smaller than a windshield is because we are supposed to spend more time looking ahead than looking back. The adage was logical, but I wasn't connecting the dots. Something had gotten cross wired inside of me during those six months.

There was a demon inside of me. I was leaving Grady at home alone, with our child, while I caroused. And she had played it straight arrow ever since we got back together. She had done her part to make the relationship work. She had gotten her old job back. She got up every morning and dropped the kid off at day care on her way to work. Then she went back to day care to fetch him as soon as she left work. When there was grocery shopping to be done, she did it, taking the kid with her and putting him in that little seat in the shopping basket. She cooked, cleaned the house, did any and everything to make the relationship work. She did her part to restore normalcy to our lives.

Meanwhile, I sank deeper into my disease. I drank heavier, stayed out longer, followed assorted women home for an endless string of one-night stands. The thing was, I didn't even enjoy myself. I surely didn't enjoy waking up every morning, feeling like my head had been caught under a road grader. And some of the broads I followed home at night were rejects from a Matamoros whore house. No wonder they hung out in bars. Otherwise, they'd never get laid.

I was driven, possessed. There was a demon inside of me. I became more demented, and in retrospect, it didn't take that long for it to happen. Finally, I crossed over the line and slapped Grady during one of our arguments. I was furious over absolutely nothing. I was out of control. I wish someone would have been there to kick me in the ass so hard, that I wore my butt cheeks as a hat.

"And if you ever, *EVER* run away from me again, I will find you, and then there is no telling what I will do. But I guarantee, you will not like it. When we have a problem, you face me and we will talk about it." I was screaming, in a fury, pointing my finger at her.

"What about now?" she cried. "You're acting like a maniac, Charley! At this point, I don't care if you kill me! If we stay together, you're going to have to get some help. I'm scared to death of you. You aren't the same person I married! I don't know who you are!"

Her words brought me to a halt. She was right. I was out of control and needed help. And so, she asked somebody that she knew for a recommendation of who would be good for the problems I was suffering, and I agreed to go. Grady went with me.

I found myself sitting on a sofa next to Grady in a small office with the door closed. The therapist, Maxine O'Reilly, wanted to know about my childhood. When I asked what that had to do with anything, she said that we "needed to get to the *root* of the problem." 'Root'? What goddamned root?

Be that as it may, before I knew what was happening, I found myself spilling my guts about all the shit that was tied up inside of me, starting from my first memories in Mexico of my father beating the crap out of my mother. There was a point where all of the pain bubbled to the surface, and I started bawling like a baby. That's the last thing I wanted to do, but once the flood started, it seemed there was nothing that would stop it. I made sounds that scared the hell out of me. Grady held me in her arms, giving me support while I purged. It was embarrassing to me, but there was no off switch!

I even talked about stuff that I didn't know was there. Things which I had been hiding from myself, such as my own culpability in Grady's disappearance. Apparently, the flap that sent her fleeing into the night, was a lot more severe than I had remembered. Still, in all honesty, I could not see justification for what she had done, or the living hell she had put me through. My outrage at that kept resurfacing. The pain I had experienced while Grady was in hiding far surpassed anything I had known up until that time, including my abortive adopted childhood and my meshuga adopted mother trying to take me out with a shotgun.

Yes, I realized that I shared in the responsibility for Grady's disappearance, and yes, I realized that I needed to get over it and move on, to turn the page. But that was going to be hard to do. It wasn't as if she had gone dark for a day or so. That would have been bad enough. But she was gone for six motherfucking, agonizing months, and it would have been longer, maybe still to this day, had I not taken proactive, albeit dangerous and illegal action to bring it to an end. I was trying. I really was. So why was I stuck? Why did the record keep replaying this same repugnant song over and over and over?

Maybe part of it was because Grady had never, not even once, apologized for dragging me through the bowels of hell. By the time Grady and the shrink got through with me, I felt like the whole stinking California fiasco had been my fault. At least, that seemed to be the way the shrink and Grady wanted me to feel. I had endured a living, white-hot burning hell for six months that came close to driving me legally insane. Did no-one want to see my side of it, even a little bit?

After a few sessions, I came to the conclusion that the whole thing was a set-up. I considered the possibility of switching to a male shrink, but then dismissed that thought. I was paying a hundred dollars an hour to be told that I needed to wipe my nose, that I had been a bad boy. The shrink sessions came to an abrupt halt. If I wanted to blame myself, I could go home and look in the mirror for free, and I didn't have somebody looking at me like I was standing on their cat's tail. Plus telling me it all started in my childhood. I didn't believe that shit for a second. My childhood was over, behind me. It had been for years.

"You're charging me a hundred dollars an hour to tell me I had a fucked-up childhood? You think I don't already know that? You think I haven't known that all of my life? This isn't a therapy session. It's a fucking parlor game, and I'm the game piece on the board. Well, the game is over." I meant it. I walked out and turned to ask Grady if she was coming with me. She looked at me, then at the shrink. Finally, she grabbed her purse and followed me out the door.

The overwhelming problem was, I loved Grady, heart and soul. I really did want to work our problems out so that we could be happy. But the help I needed, and was searching for, sure wasn't in the office of Dr. Maxine O'Reilly. By the time that little episode was over, I was more confused than ever. To say nothing of being several hundred dollars the poorer.

In hindsight, I really should have found someone, *anyone* that could have helped, and didn't have an agenda. But I didn't. I dropped the idea entirely and went wading back into the same old destructive behavior. I couldn't see it at the time, but I had an extremely serious problem. One that wasn't going to get any better on its own. In fact, like a piece of rotting wood, if you don't do something to stop the rot, it's going to keep getting worse. That is exactly what happened. My life began a downhill slide on a slippery slope, which increased in degree the longer it went on.

When I had first awakened on the island, or wherever this hell this was, I was blank. I could remember nothing, and that was torture. Had I known then what I know now, I would have left it that way. Left well enough alone and made no effort at recall. 'If I had a choice, that is. These memories that kept invading my consciousness were pointing a giant finger of guilt directly at me that was inescapable, even here. If you have a soul that is dictated to by a conscience, there is no escape. Geography or time has nothing to do with it because decency knows no borders. Your guilt will follow you, pester you, plague you. And that is what was happening to me now. Conversely, it was reassuring to know that I did have a conscience, and cared about somebody other than myself.

As more and more details of my past came into focus, I began finding myself just standing in one spot, any spot, and staring at nothing. It happened repeatedly as one memory after another came crashing in. It was approaching the point where I was actually frightened of the next recall and the guilt it would bring. I had been a disappointment to people. I had hurt people, and that is not who I wanted to be. But how does one begin to make apologies and amends from here? The term, "It's too late," never seemed more apropos, more damning.

Timing is everything. One day, as I returned to Charley Town from the beach, I spotted a large monkey making itself at home with what little stores I had gathered. It looked up and saw me coming but didn't seem particularly startled by my presence. Of course not. I was probably the first human it had ever seen. It didn't know what humans are capable of.

By now, I had a walking stick, made of bamboo, about six feet long, so I did have a weapon if it turned out that the animal was aggressive. I continued walking toward the monkey, and my stores. As I drew near, the monkey looked at me and reluctantly backed away from my stores while making a chattering sound, but did not withdraw very far. It stopped at about twenty feet, stood on all fours, and watched me, to see what I would do. What I decided to do was sit, legs folded, beside my stores. I grabbed a banana, peeled it, then offered it to the monkey.

It sat and watched me for a couple of minutes, looking at me, then the banana. After a time, it made the decision to slowly work its way toward me. That banana was just too tempting!

During our jungle style meet and greet, I noticed several things about my visitor. It was gray, a male, weighed maybe thirty-five or forty pounds, and a type of monkey known as a macaque. I don't know how I knew that, but no matter, I knew it.

The animal eventually drew near me close enough to reach out and take the banana from my hand. I expected him to quickly retreat, but he did not. He held his prize with both hands, sat on his haunches and began taking bites of his treat. This pleased me, for some reason. I had a new friend! As such, he would need a name. I decided to call him, Mac the Macaque. I wondered how long it would take him to learn his name. So, I began saying it to him.

"Hey, Mac! How you doing, boy? There ya go. Listen and get used to my voice, Mac." Mac was extremely intelligent. He watched everything I did very intently. In some instances, he duplicated what he saw. It was like the old saying, "Monkey see, monkey do!" His antics made me laugh, and after a while, when he heard my laughter, he would curl his lips back in a wide monkey grin that was hilarious.

Mac followed me everywhere. If I walked out to the beach, Mac was there beside me. If I waded into the lagoon, Mac would jump in right beside me and paddle-swim. Water did not deter him in the slightest. After a while, I actually began to train him to do things; although that was originally accidental. One day I was trying to reach a mango that was slightly too high for me. Mac scampered up the tree, walked out on the branch, grabbed the mango and dropped it down to me. I was flabbergasted. I had a buddy, a pal! One that wanted to please me!

Animals love easily. That's because they do not have a political agenda. They simply respond to the way they are treated, in a very innocent manner. Mac and I were buddies. I was no longer alone, and a lot of my apprehension seemed to dissipate. I talked to Mac constantly, about anything, realizing that he didn't know what I was saying. But it didn't matter. It was very therapeutic. Mac loved me, and I loved him back. I talked to him constantly, and he would look up at me as if he understood. He became my "Wilson."

I even made a little cot for him to sleep on beside my cot inside the hut. I didn't want him to have to sleep on the ground, in the sand. But after a night or two, he abandoned his little cot and snuggled with me. He seemed to like to push against my back as closely as he could. I was truly not alone anymore. There was at least one creature in this world that cared about me and wanted to be near me, Phil notwithstanding. Counting the parrot, I had a family!

It reached the point that when I felt a memory taking form in my mind, I pushed it away. I didn't want to remember anymore. I had been a first-class asshole, and nobody wants to be constantly reminded of their shortcomings. But that isn't how it works. My mental rejection wasn't always successful. The memories kept flooding in, despite my best efforts at rejection. And I did not like the person who was revealed, more and more with each succeeding recall.

My deprivation darkened. I went deeper into hell the more I drank. I now realize that the devil lives inside that bottle. I wish I would have realized it then. It reached a point where my morals were non-existent. There was no STOP sign when I was drunk. I drank, I whored, I gambled away my paycheck. I started getting fired from jobs and didn't give a fuck about anything. I retained enough of my sanity that I was still functional. I was a salesman, and a damn good one. So, if one company fired me, I just took my clients with me to the next place where I would manage to land a job. There is a special arrogance associated with being a drunk. They feel they are invulnerable, and infallible. I felt that for sure. I was never wrong. It was always the other guy! I was always smarter in any given situation.

Finally, I arrived at the ultimate dark place. Alcohol was making all of my decisions for me. Like all alcoholics, I was defensive and in absolute denial. I didn't live anything akin to a normal life. I did not go to work, come home at the end of the day to be welcomed by my family. I didn't long to get a kiss at the door, ask what the baby had gotten into today. Put my briefcase down and go into the kitchen to smell what was cooking on the stove. I didn't turn my attention to my child so he could show me his latest discovery. Meanwhile, he was growing, and learning how to be resentful.

But I ignored all of that. That was for the other Charley, the sane Charley, the inferior Charley! Instead, I went directly to my favorite bar by early afternoon. In my mind, I was so good at my job that I didn't need to work past noon to get everything done. Then I could embrace my hobby, sitting in a smoke-filled bar with my forearms resting against the long, dark mahogany bar, sipping my first cocktail of the day, and secretly scanning the room for any bar flies that looked lonely. Why in the hell was I doing that? I had the greatest lover in the world, right there at home, waiting for me. I knew it. I ignored it. I profaned it. Oh, God! What I would give to be able to change it!

I was wasting my life away, and in the process, ruining Grady's life. A person is allocated only a certain amount of time to live on this planet. It makes a difference what you do with that time, because, brother, there ain't no more, once that is used up! Time is no one's friend. It varies for no one or anything. It marches ahead twenty-four hours a day. And time offers no second chances. It's not like being in school where you can screw up and the teacher lets you redo your homework.

While I stayed in the bars, boozing and whoring, Grady sat at home, alone, with our child. She knew where I was and what I was doing. Why she stayed, I will never know; except that I had threatened her. I told her if she ever ran away again, I would find her and kill her. I didn't have a wife. I had a prisoner. She was miserable, and she was paralyzed.

But she had left me alone those six devastating months, when I was in absolute burning hell, goddammit! She had shown me no mercy. So let her sit home for a while! I would get there eventually. That was my 'rationale,' and it was a form of insanity.

Within a short time, I felt another memory trying to worm its way into my brain. I started screaming like a maniac. I didn't want to remember anything else. What I had remembered to this point was abhorrent. I had been a monster. I loathed who and what I had been, and I was convinced that is not who I am now. Something had changed, but I didn't know what and I didn't know when. I just knew that there had been a life altering metamorphosis, a drastic one, an epiphany, perhaps. What had brought it on? That was the memory I wanted to recapture, although I was frightened of what truth it would reveal.

"You've ruined my life, Charley. I've waited for years for you to come to your senses. All you've done is gotten worse, sunk deeper into your deprivation and self-pity." When Grady first said that, it didn't click with me. I didn't hear the truth of what I had done and was continuing to do on a daily basis. I was so self-absorbed that I could not feel somebody else's pain. But one day it hit me, and when it did, it was like a twenty mega-ton bomb. It is a shocker to get slapped in the face with that awful weapon known as 'truth'. But it was long overdue!

I didn't know who I was anymore, and I didn't care. I wasn't living a life. I was living a worthless existence, a slug on the face of the earth and society. And I was doing a miserable job, even at that. I was on a downhill plunge. No! More than that. I was on an elevator ride straight into hell. And nobody had pushed me onto that elevator. I got on it voluntarily. I wasn't in control of my life. The devil was!

At some point, I left Grady. I mercifully cut her loose. I don't know why. It was nothing she did. It was what I did. I freed her from the hell I was putting her through. Despite my insanity, she had been sticking with me, trying to be a good wife. But then, I left. One part of me said that the move was stupid beyond stupid! She was the only decent thing that had ever happened in my life. But she deserved a life too. And I had been robbing her of that.

I had pretty well run my course, meaning fucked up all of my options, and pissed off just about everybody I knew in Corpus Christi. I decided to move to Houston. Escape to a much bigger town, more options; people who didn't know me. Maybe I could start to clean up my life.

But, while looking for a place to live, I discovered that Houston was infested and infected with gangs. It is more corrupt that Chicago and Detroit combined. Murder, robbery and drugs are completely rampant there. The morning news in Houston is nothing but a body count.

So, I abandoned the plan for Houston and started drifting South, toward Galveston, looking for something along the coast. About half-way between Houston and Galveston lies a little hamlet named San Leon. It has a population of about five thousand, counting a few stray dogs. It is replete with RV parks and red-neck bars, and remarkably, some of the best seafood restaurants to be found anywhere on the Texas coast.

Ninety percent of the populous in San Leon live in beach houses. That is, if they don't live in an RV. It is a true beach-side community. It is a little spit of land that when seen from a satellite, appears to be the shape of a rose thorn on one side, which sticks off into Galveston Bay. People are very laid back in San Leon. In fact, the local newspaper touts on its banner, "A Small Drinking Community with a Large Fishing Problem." And it's very accurate!

There is some crime in San Leon, but absolutely nothing by comparison with Houston, where theft is rampant, even in the daytime, and so is murder. Overall, San Leon is a good place to live. People only get rowdy around Mardi Gras, and on the 4th of July. There are a lot of veterans who live in this little hamlet. So, they have a golf cart parade on those two holidays and dress the golf carts up like floats during Mardi Gras. There are a lot of flags on the 4th.

The 2nd most popular hang-out in town is The American Legion Post (elevated on pilings), where fishermen meet to regale each other with the latest fishing tales and of course, lie to each other. In Texas, it's called 'Bullshit,' and in Texas, bullshit is considered an art form. In fact, I would go so far as to say that in Texas, someone incapable of telling a good bullshit story is viewed as perhaps having a cognitive problem.

But everywhere, as far as the blurry eye can see, there are beach houses! Even viewed from the front deck of The American Legion Post. I like beach houses for many reasons. Among other things, the security is generally better. Thieves don't like the idea of getting caught in a place where the only escape route is to jump over a railing, down a full story to the ground, and land most likely, on cement. Or worse yet, on lawn furniture or some other obstacle.

After I bought a beach house and got settled in, my old habits returned like a hungry dog looking for a buried bone. I started hanging out in some of those red neck bars. That's when I met Marilyn, and our whirlwind affair began. The affair that ultimately led to the murder/suicide of Marilyn and Leroy. It took some time to get over that. And I couldn't sleep in the bedroom where the tragedy had occurred. Luckily, there was a second bedroom, and that's where I set up camp.

After a while, I took up with a southern belle, and, my dark side leveled off, "for a while." I actually tried playing it straight. But then, I left the southern belle because I found out that she wasn't being true to her old south culture, or true to me, for that matter, y'all! Karma, taking a bite out of my ass? She had gotten into a debauch with a character named Thomas, who had 'charmed her.' I did some research on Thomas, then went to his office to have a face to face with him. It didn't go well.

"I am Charley Flynt."

"I know who you are," he said, defiantly.

"Good. Then you know why I'm here. Leave Rose alone. Don't ever see her again."

"And what are you going to do about it, if I do?"

"What?"

He walked around his desk to where I was standing and got in my face. "Look, asshole, I know all about you. You've been in more shit than an outhouse rat. You don't deserve Rose. And I'll tell you something else, I have a lot of money. You fuck with me, and I will ruin what's left of your rag tag, miserable life. Not that there is much left. Now, get the fuck out of my office, and I mean right now."

I turned and started to leave, but paused in the doorway and said, "This isn't over, asshole. Before it is, you're going to regret those bullshit words!"

"Yeah, yeah, yeah," I heard him say, with a wave of his hand, as I departed.

But it really wasn't over. For the next few weeks, he was all I could think about. I was obsessed with coming up with some plan to cook his goose. I sat at my desk until the wee hours of the morning, thinking about things I wished would happen to him. Poetic justice would be for his pecker to go up in flames, the moment he entered Rose. I envisioned that. I focused on it. I wished it. And then, I was watching the news one morning while fixing coffee, when a very strange story started being told by the reporter.

"And in the department of bizarre, there is a report coming from UTMB this morning about a man whose... well, how do I say this? Whose 'private area' spontaneously burst into flames! And it was apparently not because of an exploding lithium battery!"

I stopped what I was doing, grabbed the remote to turn the volume up. Then, the female co-anchor identified the victim. It was Thomas. The male reporter was doing his best to maintain decorum and handle the story in a professional way, but that was difficult. He kept having to suppress a smile, and at one point apologized.

"I'm sorry, folks. I realize this is no laughing matter, to say the least." Then he tried to continue with the news report.

The inference was, the victim had experienced the anomaly at a most inopportune 'intimate' moment, and his partner had also received third degree burns because of her rather 'close proximity.' At the end of the story, the male reporter thought the control booth had cut to a commercial, when he really lost it and started cracking up. He looked at somebody off-camera and said, "Oh geez! I almost couldn't hold it. I kept thinking about how a boy-scout starts a fire by rubbing a stick in a hole!" Then he really lost it.

My knees suddenly felt weak. I sank into a chair at the kitchen table. What the hell had happened? Could it be? Impossible! But the story matched '*exactly, to the T,* what I had been obsessing about, and intently wishing for. I never in my wildest dreams thought it would come true, although to be honest, I wished beyond wishing that it would come true. I don't know if it could be called praying, but that was a close description. "There are stranger things in Heaven and on earth, Horatio!"

Through resources, meaning, friends of mine that worked at the UTMB hospital, I learned, in the days to come, Thomas's burns had been life threatening. It had been necessary to perform an operation to save his life which involved amputating the charred remains of his schlong. I was glad! The bastard had challenged me and threatened me. He had gotten his just desserts. Take that, Peckerless Thomas! And think twice next time before you threaten Charley Flynt!

Thomas was still in the hospital a couple of weeks later. I found a pay phone in a bar and called the hospital. I asked for his room. He answered after the fifth ring, and with a weak sounding voice, said, "Hello?"

I replied in a somewhat loud and triumphant voice, "What's on the special tonight, Cocksucker? Barbequed dick? I told you that you would regret threatening me. Didn't believe me, did you, punk!"

Then I started laughing uncontrollably and hung the phone up. That was the icing on the cake. Now I could put it behind me. The bad guys never fucked with Matt Dillon and got away with it. Now, nobody had better ever fuck with Charley Flynt. The consequences would be certain and severe!

CHAPTER ELEVEN

My Power Grows Stronger

I decided my beach house needed a new lid. So, I called a roofer. He came to my house, did a survey, gave me a price and we made a deal. I paid him a large deposit, in advance for him to begin work just as soon as the materials arrived. He was sort of a sullen type. But then, tradespeople are often times not happy people. Still, something inside me was trying to send me a signal.

I bought the shingles and tar paper, which the lumber yard delivered on a pallet and used a forklift to place in the fucking middle of my driveway. I could still park in my driveway, but access to the carport beneath the house was blocked. I hadn't been home when the lumberyard driver delivered the shingles, or I would have asked him to use a little courtesy and place the pallet to one side, so I could still get in. Pendejo!

Then, the delays started. The roofer, Ralph, told me he had an emergency job to do because some old widow had a damaged roof, and the rainy season was headed our way. That delay lasted three weeks, then something else came up that caused another delay. Six weeks later, the damned shingles were still sitting in my driveway, gathering dust.

I finally got Ralph to answer the phone. I told him in no uncertain terms that I was out of patience, that he needed to honor his contract and begin work on my house. I couldn't believe my ears when he answered me.

"Tell you what, Charley, go stick those shingles up your ass. I'm not going to do your roof. Leroy was a friend of mine. I know all about what happened to him and why, you piece of shit."

"Really? What about the money I paid you? Our contract?"

"Yeah, well, I used that money to buy a new TV, and that contract was a handshake. You don't have anything on paper. So, go fuck yourself, you goddamned fornicator. Keep your dick out of other men's wives."

With that, the phone went dead. I was livid. I drove to where Ralph was working, and spotted him on the high roof of a beach house. It would be risky to confront him because there was no doubt a fight would break out. I wasn't sure how good shape I was in and besides, somebody was sure to call the cops. I would wind up in the slammer. Pay a fine. Nothing would be accomplished.

So, instead, I concentrated, closed my eyes and made sure I had the image recorded in my mind's eye. Then I left.

At home, I sat at my kitchen table and began to focus; concentrate very hard about Ralph up on that steep roof, tripping and falling head-first to his death on the concrete driveway below. I focused intently. I clenched my fists and squeezed my eyes tightly shut.

After doing this for as long as I could, I took a break and went to the fridge for a beer. As I strolled out to the back deck of my house to enjoy my cold beer, I heard sirens in the far distance, coming roughly from the direction of the house where Ralph was working. It didn't take long for the news to spread like wildfire on social media, about a roofer that had somehow tripped while on a roof and plummeted to his death. "Gotcha," I thought with a smile as I sipped my cold beer. Another asshole bites the dust.

As time passed, the realization that I possessed such a bizarre and deadly power did not go to my head. But it did give me more confidence, and that confidence changed my attitude. I felt like I could conquer the world. And that affected my outward actions. I began to change, for the better. My positive attitude was reflected in my interactions with people. I didn't feel like such a victim anymore, such as I had with Grady. I stopped drinking except for an occasional beer.

And so, I began to look and act like a winner. It was reflected in everything I did. My sales almost tripled in a year. I started making good money (again!). I made new friends. People gravitated toward me, and actually wanted to be around me, to do things for me. I felt alive, like a new person. But I also never forgot my ace in the hole. Fuck with the bull, get the horns! But there was also a subtle message here, 'to self'. Act like a winner, be a winner. People are drawn to positive thinking and positive actions. In that respect, a person is one hundred percent in control of their life. You even feel better physically. It is a win – win!

Which all leads to, there is one soft spot in my armor. I love animals. I always have, all of my life, I have wanted to do something really significant to alleviate the suffering of neglected, or worse yet, abused animals. Admittedly, I haven't done much in my life that benefitted anything or anyone, not even myself, before my new outlook on life. It was time for that to change. As my health and attitude improved, my desire to do something proactive to benefit all animals became a passion. And then I had a chance to buy six acres that was near a secondary road just outside of San Leon. I bought the property, then stood beside the road in front of it and imagined what I could and would do with it.

In my mind, I began to see a no kill animal shelter taking shape. My fantasy was evolving into the realm of possible reality! Things don't just happen by themselves. Somebody has to make them happen!

The facility would be a non-profit, but first, I would have to get it built. I conned an engineer friend of mine into drafting some blueprints for a futuristic facility, big enough to house several hundred animals. Normally, those blueprints would cost a few thousand dollars. But he was an animal lover and wanted to do his part to bring this thing to life.

All he asked in return was that his name be on the brass plaque that would be attached to the wall beside the entrance. That was an easy promise to make!

That was a big step forward, because now I could envision what the shelter would look like, and I was on fire! All I needed to do now was raise the money. Well, not quite yet. First things first. There was still a lot of planning to do.

The next thing was to put together a budget and all the ancillary legal papers that I would need. Then I would be ready to go seek private funding. A budget is a bear! Trying to put together the thousands of numbers is like trying to beat a rhino to death with a flyswatter. Even so, three months later, we were ready!

There would be huge incentives for investor/donors. A leading one would be that donors would receive multiple tax breaks 'if' I could get the facility declared a 501c3 nonprofit. For that, I would need JoAnn, my attorney. She was an animal lover too and would probably cut me a discount on drawing up the papers, including a legal agreement for contributors. After that, I could launch an all-out campaign to raise money.

That led to the day that I met a guy named Esteban Campion. He called himself 'Chief', and he had the reputation of being able to raise money for just about anything. I set up a meeting with him and took along a couple of female associates that had gravitated to me along the way, who were of like spirit. They also had a better eye for detail than I did and acted as advisors. This included a beautiful woman named Lilly. And no, I wasn't 'doing' her. Our relationship was strictly professional. No hanky-panky. Besides, she was married and had two preteen daughters to raise. I had seen what messing around with a married woman could lead to. I had vowed, never again, Kemo Sabe! Ol' Charley was starting to clean up his act for real. At some point, you just have to grow up! In my case, it was a matter of better late than never. I had already caused too many people too much pain. I didn't want to do that anymore. I wished there was some way I could take back the things I had done. But time is non-repentant, and it doesn't allow you to be. I thought of Grady and my son. I had really let both of them down. I thought of trying to go to Corpus and see if she wanted to try again, now that I was cleaning up my act. But I procrastinated. I didn't do what my instinct was trying to tell me would be the right thing to do.

At first, I thought the initial meeting with Chief had gone well. He listened intently. He showed interest, and then began to give feedback on methods to use, and bragged about how he was the lead officer of an investment group that would be wild about my idea. I believed the sonofabitch!

But boy was I naïve! "Chief" secretly took a shine to Lilly (as he did many, *many* women)! Then, *behind my back*, he called Lilly and charmed her into an illicit relationship. An 'affair.' When I found out, I told Chief and Lilly that I protested. I admit, I wasn't very diplomatic when I told them, and rather verbally abusive to her. That turned out badly for me; it backfired and turned Chief against me. And I mean, *really* against me! And then, he turned Lilly against me, albeit with a bevy of lies.

How dare somebody challenge Chief! He was all powerful and irresistible to all women beyond comprehension to the inferior human mind! That is, that's how it was in Chief's narcissistic mind. This time, he got lucky. Lilly was naïve, unexperienced in the ways of a dedicated fornicator with a Don Juan complex, intent on screwing everything that can't outrun him.

After I pissed him off by protesting his indiscretion with my advisor, he made it a full-fledged campaign to contact many friends of mine, *behind my back*, (his modus operandi. He was very good at doing things behind someone's back!) and discrediting me by telling a litany of lies. And he was a highly skilled liar! His mission was to destroy me, and the animal shelter, and turn everyone I knew against me. I had been trying so hard to rebuild my life and stay on the straight and narrow road. This was like having a firecracker go off in my face.

Esteban Campion was a one-man wrecking ball! I was non-plussed because I couldn't figure out what his motive was. And finally, it didn't matter what his motive was. I was calling people I had known for years, and they wouldn't return my phone calls because of some manufactured horse crap that Chief had fed them. It was a nightmare. It seemed that it was a game to him, just like seducing women was a game to him. A game of conquest.

He was evil, through and through. The most purely evil person I had ever met in my entire life. I was convinced that he was a minion of the devil. And now that I was remembering him, my opinion had not changed. I still believed it.

His actions began to get to me. I did a brief background check on him and discovered that he had a litany of arrests ranging from fraud to multiple sexual assault charges. How had he gotten out of them? He had moved to Texas from Pennsylvania, so I made some phone calls to his home-town. He had been practically forced to leave there because of a long record of shady dealings, both personal and professionally. Even his own family wanted nothing to do with him. Chief was a piece of work! Worse; Chief was a piece of living shit. And by now, he was making me mad because he was an aggressive enemy, bent on my destruction.

That old me, my protective me, woke up inside of me and surfaced full force. I was determined to fight back with the most effective weapon I had. I felt I had no choice, really. My very existence and that of my animal shelter were being threatened. I began to focus on an image of Chief, and dream of what I wished would happen to him. He really deserved to be dead and disgraced at the same time.

Within a couple of weeks, Chief was pulled over by the cops for weaving down the road in that Cadillac of his. The cops found a load of fentanyl underneath his car seat and arrested him. He resisted arrest, started ranting, and pulled a gun on the cops. They shot Chief dead. Chief was a threat no more, *and* he had been discredited in the process. My power was growing stronger. My power was protecting me. My power was my constant, faithful guardian. Or at least that is what I thought it was. Later on, I found out the fentanyl had been planted in Chief's car by Lilly's husband, who was desperate for some way to get Chief away from his wife. After planting the drugs, he made an anonymous phone call to the fuzz. If my power had anything to do with what happened at all, it was with Chief's meltdown after being pulled over.

A couple of days later, a gaggle of cops showed up at my door, knocking loudly. I opened it, I am sure, looking surprised. A large, serious looking cop, dressed in a cheap suit and holding a folded piece of paper demanded, "You Charles Flynt?"

"Yes," I replied.

The cop shoved the piece of paper at me. "I'm Detective Carlos Garcia. We have a warrant to search these premises, as well as your office."

I accepted the paper, stunned. "What are you looking for?"

"Drugs. Please stand aside, Mr. Flynt."

"Drugs?" I said. "That's preposterous! Come in. Search until your heart is content. You don't even need a warrant. Just don't break anything."

"What do you think we would break, Mr. Flynt?"

The bevy of cops filed past Carlos Garcia, then me, and began to fan out inside my house.

"I'm not sure," I said. "But you look a little bit like a herd of bulls in a China closet. That determined, stupid look on your face. Those close-set eyes. That Bargain Barn, off the rack suit…"

Carlos Garcia now looked at me with contempt. Must have been something I said! Then he joined his compatriots in looking under everything that could be lifted in my house. "The Boys" spent an hour tearing my house apart, and even brought drug dogs in to sniff around, before they reached the conclusion that no drugs were there. The place looked like a hurricane had hit it. Finally, Detective Carlos Garcia walked over to where I waited in an over-stuffed chair. He had a frustrated look on his face.

"Where are they, Flynt?"

"That's *Mr.* Flynt, to you," I replied. "And where is what?"

"You know what. The fentanyl."

"Fentanyl?" I was genuinely surprised. "I don't know. Where in the hell did you get the brain fart that I had anything like that in this house, or anywhere else?"

"We have information," he said, with a snide look on his face.

"Information! Oh, really?" Now I was getting really mad. "Well, does your informant have a bright red nose and work in the circus? Your 'informant' must be high on juju beads, or have it in for me. Because I do not do drugs. I do not sell drugs. I do not have anything to do with drugs in any way. Now let me ask you a question."

"What?"

"Who the fuck is going to put this house back together? You goddamned apes have turned an orderly home into a rat's nest."

"Sorry about that."

I looked at him, steaming by now. "No, you're not. Now *you're* the one lying. You don't give a rat's ass what you've done here, and I intend to file a complaint."

"Do what you've got to do, Mr. Flynt. I still think you're dirty."

"Well, I'm not. You can search until your IQ increases, which I am sure will take several years."

"If you're as clean as you say you are, would you be willing to take a lie detector test?"

"Damned right, I will. And will you be willing to take one after I do, to find out if your mother and father were married when you were born?"

Carlos Garcia came close to losing it. His body language became defensive, and he half yelled, "Hey! That's enough!"

"No. I don't think it is, you sonofabitch," I said insolently. "Here I am, having to prove my innocence, when you don't have one fucking scrap of evidence against me, and…"

"How do you know we don't?"

"Because there is none to have, asshole. Now, where do we have to go to take this fucking polygraph test? I want to do it right now, so I can wave the results in your stupid looking face and prove to you what a fucking idiot you are."

"It's in Galveston."

"Fine. Lead the way."

"We'll take you."

"Fuck you! Like hell you will. I ain't going anywhere with you, bub. And when this polygraph is over, I'm going to whatever office I need to, and file a complaint against your ape ass. I'll also have my attorney file a lawsuit for damages to my house. Then I'm leaving. I'm not going to 'hang around' for some kind of red-neck witch hunt questioning, you stupid, *stupid* sonofabitch!" Then I started yelling at him in Spanish, telling him basically the same thing. That really caught him off guard, because such things sound more intense in Spanish. I ended my tirade with the word, "Pendejo," Which in Spanish means stupid beyond belief.

I headed out the door, and held it open for the bevy of cops to exit my house. Then I closed and locked the door, turned and bounded down the steps. Downstairs, cops were getting in their cars and slamming doors. They began starting their motors and to pulling out of the driveway. They had blocked the entire street, assholes! Did they think they were Gangbusters, or somebody?

I followed Carlos Garcia for the thirty-minute drive to the Galveston Sheriff's Office. Detective Garcia had apparently radioed ahead, because the polygraph was set up and a technician/examiner was waiting, prepared with a list of questions.

The examiner hooked me up with gadgets on my fingers, a blood pressure cuff looking thing on my arm, and even a kind of belt around my chest. I felt like an astronaut getting ready for blast-off.

Questions about drugs were expected, but then he caught me slightly off guard when he changed the subject.

"Did you know a Mr. Esteban Campion, nicknamed Chief?"

"Yeah, I knew the motherfucker. What's that got to do with this?"

"I'll ask the questions here, Mr. Flynt. How well did you know him?"

"A lot more than I wanted to. He was one of the weirdest, most evil people it has ever been my misfortune to know."

"Were you aware that he is dead?"

"Bacliff and San Leon are small towns. Everybody knows."

"How do you feel about his death?"

I looked at the examiner. "That's a peculiar question. I don't see what any of this has to do with whether or not I have anything to do with drugs."

"Answer the question."

"Okay, make no mistake. I'm glad he got shot. I think the cop who popped him should get a star on his Mother Goose chart. Now, this session is over! I don't know what you're up to, and I doubt very seriously that you do either. Get this shit off of me, right now!"

The examiner didn't move quickly enough. He paused to peer toward the one-way glass, where I was sure we were being watched from the other side. So, I stood up and ripped off the belt around my chest, as well as the gadgets attached to my fingers and the blood pressure cuff. I was furious. After disencumbering myself from the trappings of the polygraph machine, I opened the door of the small room, stormed out, and went looking for Detective Carlos Garcia. I didn't have to look very far. He had been watching us through the one-way glass.

I marched up to him, barely able to control myself. "Okay, what the fuck is going on here? And I mean, *really* going on?"

Garcia indicated an office door just down the hall from where we were. I followed him, he opened the door and motioned for me to go in. Befuddled, but curious, I entered and sat at a table. Garcia sat across from me.

"Okay," I said. "Here we are, all cozy. I want some answers. I've been treated like some kind of a criminal. You assholes pushed your way into my house, leaving it in shambles without so much as an apology, and now this shift of gears. I think I deserve some answers. I repeat, what the fucking hell is going on?"

Detective Garcia looked me in the eye. "How well did you know Chief?"

Now I was over the top pissed. "I thought we covered this," I hissed. "Why are we chewing our cabbage twice?"

"Just before the officers shot him, he kept yelling your name."

"So? That's a little odd, but so what?"

"When people do things like that, there is always a reason."

I couldn't imagine what he was talking about. "Let me get this straight; you are expecting me to divine the reason some evil cock sucker was saying my name! Really? I am supposed to know what is on some idiot, crazy bastard's mind, just before you popped him?"

"What was between you two?"

As mad as I was, I figured his question was reasonable. Besides, I was blistering mad at Chief, even though he was dead. So, I spent the next ten minutes telling the detective about the abortive relationship between Chief and myself, starting with, "We were enemies." Then I carefully detailed his perversion, his obsession with pussy and Lilly in particular, and the attempts to wreck her marriage; then his evil hatred toward me and efforts to ruin me. I also told the detective to check Chief's arrest record for corroboration of what I was telling him.

When I finished, Detective Garcia sat there for several moments, absorbing what I had said. Then he rose from his chair an extended his hand for me to shake. I refused the gesture. I got up and stormed out the door. "Give me a call when the girl scout cookie sale begins," I said. "Maybe I'll buy some chocolate mints from you. By the way, you need to zip up your pants."

Carlos Garcia quickly looked down and found out I had fooled him. When he looked back up at me, he was angry. I slammed the door on the way out, leaving Detective Garcia in the small room by himself. Then I returned to San Leon.

The fact was, I had been telling the truth. I didn't know a damn thing about Chief or his drug dealings, although the drugs didn't particularly surprise me. Evil motherfucker! And I hadn't had enough time to put the whammy on him, although I was mad as hell at him, and had every intention of doing so. Had things continued like they had been going, I would have gladly cooked him.

Then it hit me; were my 'special abilities' reaching critical mass? That is to say, were they boiling over and taking on a life of their own? That was impossible! Or was it? I picked up the phone and called a maid service to come put my house back together.

CHAPTER TWELVE

Meanwhile, Back on The Island

My pants were starting to look pretty ragged. I tried to carefully cut the legs off with the cutlass to make them into shorts. That was successful, pretty much. I hadn't managed to cut the legs to exactly the same length, and the cuffs (as such) where I cut were tattered. But even so, the pants were the worse for wear. It wasn't going to be very long until I would be naked if I didn't figure out a way to make some britches, or at least a loin cloth. But what could I use as material?

First of all, I hadn't seen any fur-bearing animals large enough to use their pelt the whole time I had been here. And even if I did, I doubted I could bring myself to kill them, regardless of how bad the need. That didn't seem like a very rational survival philosophy to me. After all, the situation at hand was rather dire and justified making departures from something I would normally not do. Be that as it may, I didn't want to kill unless my life was on the line.

Maybe the palm trees could supply the answer. That same interwoven fiber I used as fire punk, that was located around where the fronds emanated from the bole, might work. I didn't want to try climbing any of the tall trees, but there were plenty of young trees scattered around that were only a few feet high at the point where the fiber was. I harvested an armful of the fiber and took it to Charley Town where I began experimenting.

It didn't take long for me to discover that I was no tailor. But I managed to assemble overlaying plies of the fiber to the point that I created 'something' akin to a loin cloth. To say it was crude was an understatement. My estimate was that it wouldn't last more than a few days, and I would have to hold it in place with my belt. Then I would have to make another one, just like I had to keep placing new banana leaves on my cot. Maybe practice would make me better. "Maybe!" I certainly hoped so. And Lord, what I would give for a clean pair of undies! Mine had bit the dust long ago. They lay, like some discarded dead body, on the sand, among the brown, dried palm fronds in the palm jungle. They never even got a decent burial. Sigh! "Here lies Charley's undies. They spent their life living in the dark and supporting a couple of nuts!"

Meanwhile, my survival skills were improving, and I discovered a new food source. The fish trap, which I had positioned in the delta of the lagoon, had somewhat measured success thus far. But while trying to weigh it down with stones, I discovered (beneath the rocks) a huge version of a shrimp! It was a fresh-water prawn and was strange looking to be sure. It was like a mix between a shrimp and a lobster, but with elongated, skinny claws. The creatures were gigantic. It only took two or three to make a meal. And to say they were delicious was the understatement of the day. They tasted almost like they were buttered!

My nutrition seemed to be pretty well balanced. For 'meat', as such, I had prawns, an occasional fish, and all the gigantic coconut crabs I could possibly eat. I also had fruits in the form of bananas, mangos, coconuts, breadfruit... was breadfruit a fruit? Oh well. And, well, for the moment, that seemed to be all. But I kept smelling figs each time I made a journey up the mountainside, so I knew they had to be there somewhere. It's just that most of them were in pretty high trees, and I wasn't sure the risk was worth the reward. I kept seeing that old skeleton with the shattered femur.

But I digress! I was losing weight. My pants, as ragged out as they were, reminded me of just how much weight I had lost. When I first woke up here, they fit perfectly. Now, I had to take the belt up several notches to keep them on.

So, from a survival standpoint, I was doing pretty well. A lot better than expected. But the nagging questions, where was I? And how did I get here, never left me. Never gave me peace, not for a blessed moment! The questions were always there, tugging at my elbow, and justifiably so. Finding the answer might offer a key to escape. I began to ponder the idea of building a raft. There was certainly enough bamboo around that I could cut for material.

My reverie was interrupted by the appearance of dark blue clouds moving in from offshore. It looked like I was about to find out how waterproof my roof was. I moved my little bird, Phil, and Mac into the hut and held my breath. I briefly thought, maybe I should close the window! But of course, there was no way to close it. I made a mental note to jerry-rig some kind of shutter, and maybe even a door.

When the rain came, it did so preceded by a powerful wind that lasted at least five minutes and blew the hell out of everything. Lightning and rolling thunder completed the package. My hut held, but the lean-to I had constructed after my first night here, disappeared. Palm fronds flew everywhere, and fruit from the nearby mango tree fell from the tree, carpeting the ground. I also heard many coconuts hitting the ground with a thump. If I lived through this storm, I would eat good mangos and coconuts, at least for a few days!

Then, the rain came. It did not fall gently, like in a song, but rather pounded down like it was trying to flood everything. Luckily, my roof, for the most part, was holding. At least for the moment. There were a couple of small leaks. But under the circumstances, I could hardly believe there weren't more. My little family and I huddled against the storm and waited in fear for it to pass. I thought of the skeleton in the cave. Is weather such as this the reason he had sought a cave for shelter?

After about an hour, but what seemed like forever, the rain began to abate. Then, it stopped as suddenly as it had begun. There was rolling thunder that walked across the sky as if the storm was saying goodbye. Then the sky began to lighten. I went outside, Mac at my side, to survey what the storm had left behind. Wet, is what it had left! Everything was soaked through and through. The waterfall had almost doubled in size because of the water left on the mountainside.

My iron pot hadn't gone anywhere because of its weight. But now it was filled to the brim with rainwater and debris. My campfire, which I tended so carefully, and never allowed to die, was now a puddle of black ashes. Not only that, but anything I would use to make a fire was soaked. No hot water for a bath, and no cooked food until I managed to find some dry tinder from somewhere. I was disappointed, but not devastated. Somehow, it seemed to be part of the program around here. "Survive on an island: plan on getting wet once in a while! And/or kicked in the ass once in a while!" I'd have to remember to write that passage when I put my memoires together, someday!

Mac the macaque wasted no time in making his way to the cornucopia of mangos, and digging in. I laughed when he looked at me, half eaten mango in his hands, and mango smeared all over his face, looking like a kid in a candy store. I also peeled one and placed it into Phil's cup, then moved him from the perch inside the hut, to the wet one outside, where his mango waited.

Seeing Mac with the mango smeared face reminded me of my son, when he was still a baby, before he grew up and became recalcitrant, angry and resentful of everything around him, especially me. When he made it into junior high, I constantly received phone calls from the school principal complaining about one thing or another.

"Mr. Flynt, we caught your son super gluing schoolbooks to the walls in the hallway!" But even when he was only a few years old, he showed signs of meanness. We got him a kitten, thinking that a pet might give him something to love and care for. He slammed the kitten down on the cement porch in front of our house, killing it. I tried to tell him that was wrong, that he was supposed to love animals and treat them with kindness. He looked up at me with a cold stare that is hard to describe.

I took him fishing. But when we caught a fish, he began beating it with a stick that he found. By the time I got to him to take the stick away from him, the fish was a bloody mess. I threw the carcass into the water and put my son in the car and drove home.

I couldn't do anything with him, and neither could Grady. Finally, we both gave up and sent him to live with his aunt. Maybe she could do something with him, although I seriously doubted it. Granted, I was not a very good father. I tried. I guess I just didn't try hard enough. I was shooting into the dark. I didn't know what a 'good father' was supposed to do, especially when there were problems. I had no examples to draw from. And fatherhood did not come naturally to me. I don't know if it does to anybody. Was there supposed to be a built-in parental instinct? One that came with the kit? If so, it got left out of the kit they gave me.

All I could remember was fleeing down the street as fast as my legs would carry me, trying to outrun being shot by a wigged-out mother. There was no father present that day to grab the shotgun and stop the bitch's rampage. What is it that a father was supposed to do? And then of course, there was the old bruja in Mexico and her admonition that the kid would grow up to be my enemy. Seems like she knew what she was talking about, because things were sure shaping up to be that way.

Enough reverie. Right now, I needed to make the most of the mango bonanza and also tackle the biggest problem, that of how to restore my fire. Everything was wet. There was no easy solution. Maybe no immediate solution at all. I would just have to wait a few days for things to dry out a bit. It was frustrating, to say the least.

Then it occurred to me that one rainstorm might just be the beginning. Maybe this was the beginning of the rainy season. Were there rainy seasons wherever this was? If so, I was in for a pounding, perhaps almost daily. If that was the case, I had a problem. I simply was not prepared or equipped for such an event. Not in any way. If I wanted to continue to survive, I was going to have to come up with some way to counter the problem. For a brief moment, I pondered moving up the mountainside to the cave. But I kept seeing that shattered leg, and finally dismissed the idea.

Necessity is the mother of invention. Since I was so obviously exposed to the possibility of what 'might' come, survival dictated that I do something to make preparations. But what preparations? First, analyze the problem. 1. Marginal roof. It held through this rainstorm, but how much more can it take? 2. Campfire. Needed for cooking and comfort amenities. 3. Dry fuel for the fire. Where and how to store it to keep it dry. The analysis was simple. I had three problems. And if I wanted to add the most obvious one, that of rescue, or God help me, escape from this place, that would bring the number to four. Sadly, at this point, number four seemed like an extremely remote possibility. I had even given up on sweeping my HELP rocks on the beach. It sounded frighteningly like capitulation. It felt that way too, if I let the emotion in. I had pretty much resolved myself to a fate here on the island… or whatever this place was!

Admittedly, I wanted to see an end to this wonderful little vacation in paradise. But daily visual searches of the horizon had been fruitless. Not once had I seen any silhouette of a ship, no matter how distant. I never once saw a contrail of an airplane flying overhead. I saw no flotsam on the beach that would give hope of being somewhere reasonably close to shipping lanes. I mean, some things, such as some plastic junk has the reputation of traveling for hundreds of miles before succumbing and sinking to the bottom. But there was nothing. Not one blessed thing! Ever! This was the most pristine beach on the planet!

The only evidence I had found of any humanity, past or present, had been the skeleton of an old pirate. At least I surmised that he had been a pirate, judging from the remnants of his clothing. I really didn't want to devote thought to how frapping strange all of this was. But it was there, and undeniable. Like a shadow lurking from behind the bole of a palm tree, watching me, amused at my consternation.

How had I gotten here? No evidence. None! As in, Nada! Just me and a pristine beach, a pristine jungle, a pristine lagoon... a pristine ocean that stretched to the pristine horizon. I hit emotional overload. Despite memory recall about much of my life, those moments leading up to my arrival on the island were still somewhere behind some kind of a mental cloud. My frustration was beyond measure, because I couldn't let go of the idea that knowing how I got here held the key to how I would leave.

Suddenly and without warning, incredible fear gripped me like I had never felt before. It wasn't just emotional, it was physical. I had never really understood what the term "fear gripped me," meant before this moment. And I felt alone. So very alone! I started gasping for air, I became weak and fell to my knees. It was everything I could do to keep the last remnant of hope from abandoning me. I stayed there on my hands and knees, unable to move for close to an hour.

At last, the paralyzing feeling began to dissipate. Eventually, I struggled to my feet, bracing myself against an adjacent palm tree for several minutes. Then I staggered back to my hut, where I could sit on my cot and recover for a while. Recover, and try very hard to not think. One thing was becoming very clear, 'thinking' brought me no relief, only emotional turmoil.

I tried to hide from myself by becoming busy. When I had explored the Yucatan and studied the Maya Indians, I was always a bit amazed that they built their stick houses in an oval shape, and always, always, had a cook-fire built in the smack dab middle of the house. That way, when it rained, their cook fire was protected.

I took a lesson from that memory and set about constructing a large palapa. When complete, I would move my fire pit to the center of it. I even copied the Maya style of making walls by cutting small poles which I stuck into the ground a few inches, then affixed the opposite ends, the 'tops' to the horizontal joists/rafter supports. Or at least, the island version of joists. This was a good method because it lent additional strength to the joists, which would keep them from sagging when the weight of rafters and palm fronds were added. Finished size was not an oval, but rather, a square, measuring about 20' by 20'. By comparison, it dwarfed my hut.

Building the Maya style structure took several days. I didn't count the number of days, because it didn't matter. Time was measured differently here. In fact, to a great extent, time lost all meaning. Eventually, I got around to rolling the old cast iron pot from its place beside the lagoon, to a spot close to the center of the palapa. Then I built a palette out of bamboo logs, where I could stack firewood a few inches above the ground. I didn't know how much good that would do, but it was worth a try.

Next, I filled the pot with water. This was going to entail more work, being farther away from the lagoon. But what the hell! Then I stacked the driest wood I could find, tightly against the old pot. I wouldn't be able to use the eyeglasses to start a fire here, since the pot and wood were shaded by the palapa. So, I gathered up some punk, made a small stack in a sunny place beside the palapa, and finally got a plume of smoke started. I carefully blew on it until I had a flame, then quickly moved it to my main stack which surrounded the pot. Luck was with me. I had my heating fire started again. Tonight, I would take a nice warm bath, and eat a hot, cooked supper! Then came the surprise!

That night, I was miserable. The rain had spawned more mosquitos. I had to completely wrap myself in banana leaves and lie in a fetal position on my cot. Usually, smoke from my cook fire acted as a pretty effective repellent, but not tonight. Tonight, they were voracious.

CHAPTER THIRTEEN

Getting Back on Track

After the 'Chief' fiasco, I decided that I needed to get back on track with the one thing that really meant something to me. So, I got busy and found an engineer and designer to work up a budget for me on the animal shelter. That would be the very first thing I needed before I could go on a fund-raising safari. Animals were my passion. And I did not want to limit my efforts on their behalf to just the shelter. I needed to be able to hire a lawyer to draft a law which made animal abuse of any kind a felony, with penalties severe enough that it would make some creep who was a potential abuser, think twice about his/her actions before raising a hand to an animal. And then I needed a lobbyist who believed in my goals to help me raise enough hell in Austin to get the law considered and attached to an agenda.

It took some time, but at last, I had a thirty-page fine-line budget in my hands. Now I needed to teach myself how to go about raising money while I had to tell people there was absolutely no chance of making a monetary profit on whatever they invested. Seemed like it was going to be a hard sell. But I was determined to get this shelter built. If there was one decent microbe about Charley Flynt, this was it. Thinking about it, there wasn't anything I was trying to prove at all. And there was no profit motive. I just wanted to build my animal shelter and bring sanctuary to unloved creatures.

When I watched television and saw any PSA seeking new members for one animal help organization or another, I couldn't watch when they showed footage of a suffering animal. It broke my heart. Animals are so innocent. They cannot understand why some human would punish them, or abandon them on the side of the road. And I didn't understand either. But I had wanted to make it my life's work to help stop it. Now, maybe I could bring my sales abilities, and my advertising knowledge to fore in a quest for the betterment of the creatures I loved.

I sat at my desk at home and looked at the bottom line of the budget. Ten point two million dollars! Where in the fuck was I going to come up with that kind of money? Hey-soos marimba! Talk about biting off a big wad to chew! But, building that shelter was more than a goal; it was a destiny. *My* destiny! Countless animals were out there that needed help. And by God, I was going to give it to them!

A little over a year later, I had reached my monetary goal! Nobody was more amazed than I was! I had the 10.2 mil! As it turned out, it hadn't been as hard as I had thought. It took a hell of a lot of legwork, and some airplane rides, but I did it! Getting big shots to hand me large sums of money was simple once I told them I had formed a 501c3, and everything they gave me was a legal deduction from their taxes. They loved that. There's nothing rich people love more than having a legal chance to fuck the government when they feel like the government has been fucking them without mercy for years.

Now, I was ready to begin construction. I bought a portable building and had it set up on site. Then put it together as an office, complete with land lines, computers, bookkeeper and secretary. Pre-production planning took a conference table full of construction engineers and materials experts about a month, but one fine spring day, we had a ground-breaking ceremony at the construction site. The mayor of San Leon was there to stick the golden shovel into the symbolic dirt, as well as other regional potentates, even including a senator! Reporters from the local newspapers were there, plus two of the TV stations from Houston.

"We're here, in sunny San Leon, talking with Mr. Charles…"

"Charley."

"What?"

"I would prefer Charley, not Charles. Charles is too formal. I'm not a formal kind of guy."

"Oh, sorry. We're talking with Mr. Charley Flynt, founder and CEO of a new ultra-modern facility for homeless animals. Mr. Flynt has named his facility, *L'il Critters*. What would you like to tell us about L'il Critters, Charley?"

"I'm very proud of this undertaking, designed to better the lives of many distressed, abused and homeless animals. This will be a no-kill shelter. We will have veterinarians on staff at all times to oversee the medical and health needs of our animal wards. Our ultimate goal will be to find forever homes where animals will be safe and secure and loved. Therefore, our adoption process will involve careful screening of all prospective critter parents. While animals are in our care, they will be treated with the utmost dignity, respect, care, proper feeding and attention that we can give them, plus daily activity by volunteers."

The reporter warmed up to me and the topic, and it was a good interview, as were the stories that appeared in the various local newspapers. And me? I was as busy as a one armed paper hanger, overseeing the tiniest aspect of construction. Somebody accused me of 'micro managing.' I told him to kiss my micro ass. Nothing about this facility was going to be left to chance. Every goddamned detail, no matter how small, would be brought under the microscope to make sure it was done right. Anybody who didn't share that philosophy and goal could get the fuck out!

It took a year, but at last the construction was almost complete. Only a few punch outs remained. I was tired. Tired deep inside but feeling great. I think that moment was the happiest I have ever been. Then the phone rang. It was Dave, a friend of mine.

"Hello!"

"Charley, I just wanted to offer my condolences. I am so sorry. I want you to know, I'm here, if there's anything I can do for you."

"Condolences? What condolences? What for?"

There was a long pause on the phone. Finally, "Oh my God! You haven't heard. I don't know what to do here. I shouldn't be the first one to tell you."

"What the hell are you talking about, Dave?"

Another pause. "It's Grady. She's passed away. I saw it on Facebook."

Dave kept talking, but I have no idea what he said. I was dumbstruck numb. I stood there with the phone in my hand until I started shaking uncontrollably. Suddenly time lost all meaning. I managed to stagger to the nearest chair and sag down into it. Why had nobody in my family called me and told me? I needed to talk to my son and find out if this was true. But I hadn't talked to him in years. I didn't know his telephone number.

I had to pay to find it. I was shaking so hard that I misdialed several times before I entered the right numbers. At last, I heard the phone ringing. Three rings and he answered.

"Hello?"

"This is your father."

"Yeah, so what the fuck do you want?"

I just heard the awful news. Is it true."

"Yeah, it's true."

"How did it happen?"

"What the fuck do you care?"

"I care. I love her. I have always loved her."

"Yeah, right! You want to know 'how it happened'? You murdered her, you worthless sonofabitch. That's what happened."

"What?"

"She loved you. I can't imagine why. You shit on her in every way a man can shit on a woman and you did it for years... *years*! She pined for you. She cried for you. She wouldn't listen to reason when I tried to tell her to forget you and get herself a real man. After all those years, she gave up inside. She just gave up. You could see it in her eyes. She had always hoped you would regain your sanity, or something, and come home. Instead, you moved hundreds of miles away to East Jesus, or somewhere, and left her completely isolated. So, her heart gave out. She just wanted to die." He started bawling. "She wanted to die, and it's your fault! You lousy bastard!"

"When is the funeral? I want to be there," I said.

It took him several moments before he could speak. At last, "Fuck you! I'm not going to tell you where it is or when it is. And if by some chance, you do show up, I'm gonna blow a hole in you big enough for an eagle to build a nest in. I swear it."

I pressed the button and ended the call. I sat there, until daylight turned to dark. There was ringing in my ears that I was almost thankful for because the sound made it harder to concentrate. It seemed like I had only been sitting there a few minutes when the sun started to come up and the phone started ringing. It was various people from the building site. I responded by telling them I would be there shortly. I wasn't sure I could function. My mind and heart were wracked with guilt and pain. My son was right. I had murdered Grady. My guilt was fathomless. This negated any self-delusion I had about me being an okay person because of L'il Critters. Nothing could take away this shame, or the awful truth behind it.

After some time passed, I found the strength to get up out of the chair and stagger down the steps to the car. At the nearly completed animal shelter, comments were not good. I was trying to take care of business, but I just couldn't concentrate.

"Hey, Charley, you get caught underneath a steam roller?"

"Hey, man! You look like refried dog shit!"

"Charley? Is that you? Good grief, man, you look like a zombie. What did you do, comb your hair with a leaf blower?"

"Run out of razor blades, Charley?"

I found a moment to escape and drove to one of San Leon's most backwater, hard to find red-neck bars. I left my phone in the car and over the next few hours, proceeded to get completely blitzed. Then, I tried to drive home, but that did not end well. Cops pulled me over after I creamed no less than two stop signs. I remembered nothing. I woke up in the slammer hours later, my head feeling like I would have to die before I could get any better.

I managed to struggle up off the bunk and staggered to the bars. "Where am I?"

A deputy in the adjacent room looked up from what he was doing and said, "Isn't that kind of obvious? Look around. This ain't Disney World."

I rubbed my head. "How long have I been here?"

"Dunno," the deputy said. "You were here when I came on duty. You must have really tied one on. You smell like a fricking cesspool!"

At that moment, I woke up enough to remember the reason for my debauch and it hit me like a cement truck.

A wino, lying on his bunk in the adjacent cell cut a fart loud enough to crack the concrete. "Sorry," he mumbled, and fell back to sleep.

"How the hell do I get out of here?" I asked the deputy.

"Gotta see the judge so she can set bail," he replied. "You got a lawyer?"

"Yes."

"Well, if I was you, I'd use that one phone call to call 'em."

"I need a lawyer?"

"Ya think? Your blood alcohol level pegged the meter when they arrested you. You had flattened at least two stop signs and took a short cut across a guy's front yard, trying to dodge, according to you, a squirrel. When they arrested you, you told one of the arresting offers that he sucked dicks on the side for drug money, *plus*, lest we forget, you said his mother was a dockside whore in Galveston. So, yeah, I'd say you probably need a lawyer,"

"So, what's wrong with trying to dodge a squirrel?"

"At *night*, Charley? How many squirrels you see at night?"

"Well, it's still better to take out a few shrubs."

"You're lucky you didn't take out the homeowner. He had just gone into his house."

So, I called JoAnn, my attorney and told her I was in jail.

"Really? What did you do, Charley?"

"I got blasted, then tried to drive home. The fuzz stopped me."

"Predictable. I heard about Grady. I am so very sorry, Charley."

"How did you hear about it?"

"I'm your lawyer. Your son has gotten a court order prohibiting you from being at the funeral. I've been trying to reach you. That kid of yours is a piece of work."

"Yeah, I know. I should have kept my pants zipped up the night I did that deed."

"Why didn't he notify you when she was in the hospital? She was there almost a month."

"What"

"Want my opinion, Charley? I understand there is a lot of money in her estate. He's fighting hard to make sure you don't find out about it."

I thought about him denying me a chance to be by Grady's side when she was dying, because of selfish greed. My pain deepened. Could this get any worse?

"So, can you get me out of this place?"

"I'll be there in about an hour. In the meantime, try to keep your mouth shut. That arresting officer really didn't appreciate being called a cocksucker."

"I'll try," I said, and hung up.

I sat on the cot in my cell, waiting for JoAnn, and thought about what a heartless piece of shit my son had grown up to be. He was a monster. I didn't care about any money in the estate, and I certainly was not going to cheapen Grady's memory by fighting over it. I was close to hitting emotional overload. I didn't know how much more I could take. In all honesty, I was close to biting the big one. I didn't believe in suicide, but I was coming a lot closer to understanding why people did it.

Nighttime, Charley Town: I sat cross-legged atop fresh banana leaves, staring unblinking into the flames of my campfire, and remembering. I never did recover from Grady's passing. There is an old saying; you never get used to it, you just learn how to deal with it. The saying, like so many 'old wife's tales,' is unerringly true.

I never got over her death. And I would carry the guilt of what I had done to her, forever. I did not want forgiveness. I deserved to suffer. I would have at least liked to be at her bedside to tell her I still loved her and give her what comfort that I could. My son cheated me out of that, selfish bastard that he was. I would loathe him the rest of my days. Why-o-why hadn't I kept my dick in my pants that day? Regret be thy name. The old bruja in the Yucatan, so many years ago, had been right. How had she known? Moreover, why hadn't I taken her more seriously?

There really is something beyond our conscious level, a spirit world. Perhaps a parallel world. And there are those who can divine evil. Maybe because they are spirits who walk among us in disguise. Sadly, my son was the personification of evil. A minion of the devil. He was born with it in him.

What did that say about me? I was his progenitor. Was I evil too? I didn't want to think that I was. But it might be a good reason to fall on my knees and ask the Boss to cast out any evil spirits that could be hiding inside of me. I was confused, frightened, frustrated, and somewhat angry. People think that they have absolute control of their lives. But there is a lot of shit that is beyond our control. Things we never think about because 'those things have always been there.' "It" has always been there, influencing our thoughts and actions, silently, invisibly.

Sleep was difficult that night. I wasn't very happy about the memories that were coming back to me. And I couldn't shake the nagging notion that those memories somehow had something to do with my being here. It was an old story by now that kept repeating itself. But that's the way my mind works. It won't let a mystery go until I have solved it.

When I finally did wake up the next morning, my body felt like it was made out of lead. It was depression. I needed to think about something else, please!

I did not want to profane Grady's funeral in any way. The conflict with my son would do exactly that. I would stay away from the funeral, even though I felt like I was being torn asunder inside by an evil creature of my own creation. What a dichotomy! In this moment, I felt like I had been my own worst enemy the majority of my life. And as much as I wanted to resist the idea, I knew it was true. It was true! I blinked. How does someone escape from a prison of their own making?

I forced myself to return my focus to the shelter, whose name I had decided to change to 'Wag-Nation'! I wasn't sure that was better than L'il Critters, but it's what I had decided to do. Rationale and logic be damned!

It was almost finished. I needed to hire a director for the facility. It couldn't be me with all the turmoil going on in my life. After holding interviews for several days, I selected a woman named Tammy Longoria. I had known her for a while and knew her to be a devout animal lover who was intelligent and had a cool, level head. She would be good in stressful situations. What I didn't know was whether or not she had any interest in running Wag-Nation. But then she called me on the phone and asked if I had found 'my leader'. When I said not yet, she asked if she could interview. I knew in a heartbeat that I had found my director. It was like taking ten thousand pounds off of my head. I gave her carte blanche. Her word would be law, in every way. Conversely, I would stay the fuck out of the way, and let her do her job.

The facility including all finishing touches was done within a couple of weeks. Tammy had run some ads and started staffing up. I tried to watch from the sidelines, but was drawn into a few obligations. I was trying to program myself completely out of any operational responsibilities. The only part I would play would be, with the help of JoAnn, to apply for grants and other government funding, as well as seek out consistent contributors. It was one thing to create this ark. It was another thing to keep it afloat.

To that end, guided tours of the facility were a tremendous P R tool. When prospective contributors came and toured Wag-Nation, they wanted to be a part of what we had created. And that, no matter how many times I heard it, was encouraging. At last, Charley Flynt had done something right, something worthwhile, something to justify my miserable existence in this judgmental world!

We were going to be able to house close to a thousand animals at any given time. We had ultra-modern indoor runs with doors to an outside play area. All runs were accessible by a series of long hallways which had runs on both sides. We had a fully supplied and staffed veterinary clinic, a nutrition center. The lighting had been designed by a top lighting designer who specialized in restaurants! We even had a P A system where we played relaxing music twelve hours per day.

Our animal guests were fed twice per day And, that part was not animated. There were no automated food dispensers. Each animal received personal attention and encouraging words to accompany their meals. Sadly, many of the animals who came to us were derelicts. The love they received at Wag-Nation would be the first they had known in their entire lives. I was amazed at the heartlessness of some people. How could anybody not love a little animal? Especially when the animal was so willing to return that love. It is a strange world!

All standards at Wag-Nation were set very high, for veterinarian care, food, and especially sanitation. We managed to attract a lot of volunteers who would spend one-on-one time with each animal, giving them attention so they would feel loved, and not just like an inmate in some cold hearted, fancy jail. "The quality of mercy is not strained!"

We had comfortable, living room type areas where adoption applicants could meet their future pet and interact with them to make sure this was the critter for them. Employees of the facility would go to the applicant's home during the approval process and make sure the information they had provided on their application was accurate; size of home, size of yard, fenced or not, number and age of children. And above all applicants had to sign a notarized document stating that they would never, under any circumstance "Stake-out" a dog on a chain. If they were caught doing so, the animal would be seized, and they would not get it back. And if the anti-chaining law I was proposing got passed, they would automatically be charged with a crime, have to appear in court and pay a stiff fine.

Now that Wag-Nation was operational, I sat down with JoAnn and began to kick around ideas about other anti-animal abuse laws that I wanted to get passed. To that end, I picked up the phone and contacted the headquarters of the Global Humane Society. I figured an alliance with them would give me far more clout and perhaps a treasure trove of information about such laws that might short cut, timewise, what I wanted to do. The Global Humane Society was very responsive to my request and ideas. They even offered a brass plate to mount on our wall beside the entrance.

JoAnn sat in on all of these phone calls. It definitely gave her a big gun to work with. She went to work on the Wag-Nation proposed anti animal abuse laws project, so it was time to have the ribbon cutting and declare Wag-Nation officially open for business, although we were already accepting animals from multiple sources.

We brought in a professional party planner to make sure no detail was overlooked. We sent out invitations, placed ads in the local publications plus The Saltwater Angler Magazine, since it is kind of a fisherman's Bible in this seaside fishing community. We made sure every contributor received a VIP invitation. Plans were made, caterers hired, we contracted a mariachi band, and a videographer. We made sure we had several uniformed hostesses on hand to wander around with hors d'oeuvres and to refill glasses with champagne.

At last, it was time to pull the trigger! People started arriving right on time and almost before you knew it, we had an elbow-to-elbow crowd. Everyone was anxious to tour the facility from stem to stern. There were constant oohs and aahs and happy sounding comments from the visitors about never having seen a facility so well thought out and designed. I got hugs and one lady broke down and cried with gratitude. Most people wanted to know what they could do to help. And of course, I told them. Tammy told them. JoAnn told them. Some of our contributor/ board members told them. Wag-Nation was going to be an overwhelming success. Maybe even set the bar for other facilities. I confess, I felt proud. If vanity is a sin, then fuck it! I was guilty!

JoAnn came up to me and slipped her arm into mine. "You did it, Charley, you really did! This place is great! I am *deeply impressed* with some of the fine tuning you did here to make life comfier for your animal wards. Congratulations!"

I was feeling good for the first time in a long time. "Thank you, JoAnn. This has been a dream of mine for longer than I can remember.

It still seems like it's a dream. I can hardly believe it's actually here, in front of me! But it's not about me, or for me. It's about all the unloved animals in this country. I hope we have set a new standard here that will be an example of how animals deserve to be treated, and maybe influence other facilities to do the same."

JoAnn laughed softly and patted my arm. "I know you must be proud, and deservedly so."

"Yes," I said. We walked closer to the mariachi band so we could wash ourselves in the classical Mexican music.

Later that evening, the party had about run its course. Most of the guests offered a parting congratulations, and left to go home, or to dinner, wherever. I wanted one more glass of champagne, but there were no open bottles. There was, however, one unopened bottle parked on the ice. All the girls were busy doing various clean-up chores, so I grabbed the bottle and opened it myself. The bottle made the usual loud pop when the cork came out. For some reason, I didn't want to set the cork down where I might lose it, so I put it in my pants pocket. I poured my glass full of the golden liquid, took a sip, but for some reason, it didn't taste all that good to me. I sat the glass down on the server's table and walked away.

This had been a glorious day. Probably one of the best days in my life. But all I could think about was, I wished Grady could be here with me, at my side to enjoy it. My pain and guilt rushed in and almost drowned me. Even what I had done here, for the betterment of animals, would not make up for my sins, would not erase the misery I had been responsible for. Nothing would negate that, not ever. My immediate survival forced me to think of something else. It was either that or lose my mind to grief.

I went home, alone. I wanted to be completely alone, and yet I didn't. I sat in the darkness in my living-room for hours until finally, sleep took me mercifully away.

CHAPTER FOURTEEN

The Visit

I was awakened sometime mid-morning by the ringing of the phone. I was still in my chair, in the living-room. I fumbled around in my half sleep and fished the phone out of the belt saddle.

"H'lo?"

"Charley?"

"Yeah."

"I found her."

"What?"

"This is Larry. I found Grady's grave."

Suddenly, I sat up straight in my chair. "Are you sure?"

"Yep. No doubt about it. She's at the Mesquite Cemetery in Corpus Christi."

"Jesus, Larry. I owe you. Thank you *very* much!"

"You want me to drive you down there?"

"No, thank you. There's no time."

I managed to get up out of my chair, unsteady as I was. I didn't stop to do anything. I didn't brush my teeth, comb my hair, shave. I just headed for the front door and down the stairs. I stopped at the nearest gas station and nervously filled my tank. I didn't think to retrieve my credit card and put it back in my wallet, which I had placed on top of the gas pump. I just stuck the fuel hose back in its cradle, got in my car, and took off, making a hard left onto the street and getting honked at by some guy I had cut in front of.

Larry Ackerman was a private detective that I had once designed some advertising for. I devoted a lot of time in preparation of his ads and commercials The advertising that I designed for him worked and his business flourished. We had been friends ever since. He had once made the comment that he owed me a favor, and if I ever needed anything… so, I had called in that favor, and Larry had come through like a champ.

Four hours later, I entered the outskirts of Corpus Christi. I was nervous. My palms were sweating. I knew where the Mesquite Cemetery was. It was on the opposite side of town, so I had at least thirty minutes more to get there.

Once at the cemetery, I cruised slowly around, looking for new gravesites. It was a fairly small cemetery, so it didn't take long to spot one that looked brand new. I parked, got out of my car, leaving the keys in the ignition, and walked nervously over to the grave where I read the headstone. It was hers. I tried to read it, but I got no farther than Grady Flynt. Then, the tears made it impossible to read any farther.

I fell on my knees beside the grave and sobbed. The pain wracked me. I shook uncontrollably. Somewhere in my blubbering, I managed to say, "Grady, I am so, so sorry for everything I did to you. I would give anything to go back in time and change things, to do it right. To honor you the way you deserved to be honored and loved."

I could say no more. There was nothing left inside of me. I just wanted to sit there and be close to her. And so, I did that. I don't think that I could have moved if I tried.

I don't know how long I sat there in reverie. Time meant nothing. I reflected on the many ways I had fucked up in my life. And that would have been alright if my actions had just affected me. But that wasn't the case. I had hurt people. People had died. And it was my fault. I cursed time, because time is merciless. It allows for no mistakes, no regrets, and it certainly does not shift into reverse to grant second chances.

I was numb. I reached out and rubbed the dirt on top of her grave. That's when I noticed the brown shoed feet standing on the opposite side of the grave. I looked slowly upward until I saw my son's face. He had no moustache, but one of those beards that start at the chin and cover the neck and throat.

"Can't you afford a razor?" I asked. "Or is it that you're just too fucking lazy to shave?"

"Hello yourself!" he replied.

I looked back at the grave. "I loved her. I did a piss poor job of it, but I loved her."

"I told you not to come here."

"Did you really think you could keep me away? All I want to do is pay my respects. Don't worry about me finding out about the money. I know about it, and I don't give a shit. I have no plans of profaning Grady's memory with a goddamned cat fight over an estate. Keep the money, you asshole. Just let me be with her and say goodbye, pay my respects."

"Well, pay 'em!"

I started to get up from where I sat, beside the grave.

My son said, "Don't bother getting up, because I'm fixing to kill you."

"Why bother?" I said. "I'm already dead inside."

"Well now, you're going to be dead on the outside!"

I didn't care. I looked up at him just in time to see his hand come out from behind his back. He was holding a large pistol that looked like a Glock. He pointed it at my head and pulled the trigger. I momentarily heard the explosion and felt the impact of the bullet against my forehead. Then there was nothing. There was blackness. I was falling.... falling... falling

CHAPTER FIFTEEN

New Beginning

"I awoke to the sound of strange birds. Even before I opened my eyes, I knew something was wrong!"

I stood beside my hut, remembering my first moments of consciousness on the island, or 'here'. I raised my hand to my forehead to see if there was a hole, then rubbed my face. As I rubbed my chin, it hit me. I only had a one-day beard! I had been in this place for months. I should look like Rip Van Winkle by now. But I didn't! I had never thought about it before this moment. Then I felt my head. Same result. I did not need a haircut. My fingernails hadn't grown. Everything was the same as the first moment I woke up here.

So, did that mean…? Yes, it must! Was I dead? The gunshot! My own son murdered me! So, where was this place? As in *"where"* was this place REALLY? Would I be here forever? Was this place really a part of the world, or was it on a grain of sand? Would I age? What about the old skeleton in the cave? Who had he been? Had he started out like me?

Was this it? I am here, alone? Forever? Forever and forever? And what about hope? What about music?

Hundreds, thousands of questions were surfacing, like skyrockets exploding on the Fourth of July. My mind went numb, into overload. Everything seemed so quiet. I didn't hear the sound of the distant waves washing up on shore. The birds fell silent. The implications were... fathomless. However, it seemed I would have plenty of time to divine the answers, one at a time, at my leisure.

I turned and walked to the beach, Mac at my side. I had no expectations of seeing a passing ship. It was now crystal clear. My ship had already sailed!

ABOUT
GEORGE DISMUKES

George Dismukes has pursued bullfighting and professional snake-milking, chasing wild animals across the Seregeti in the movie business, and operating an animal-export company in Peru. He spent many years exploring archaeological sites of the ancient Maya Indians in Central America and studying their lost civilization, at one point living in Honduras. He founded a video-production company in Houston, which led to a CLEO award for his PSA work. His hobbies include growing exotic chili peppers and experimenting with salsa recipes. Above all, George is a devout animal lover with two dogs, Pulga and Gizmo. George lives on the Texas Coast with his soulmate and closest friend, Nadine, where he writes and works in magazine advertising.

Contact George at mayanartintl@yahoo.com, and please leave those 5-star reviews where you bought the book and beyond.

Fresh Ink Group
Independent Multi-media Publisher

Fresh Ink Group / Push Pull Press

Voice of Indie / GeezWriter

✄

Hardcovers

Softcovers

All Ebook Formats

Audiobooks

Podcasts

Worldwide Distribution

✄

Indie Author Services

Book Development, Editing, Proofing

Graphic/Cover Design

Video/Trailer Production

Website Creation

Social Media Marketing

Writing Contests

Writers' Blogs

✄

Authors

Editors

Artists

Experts

Professionals

✄

FreshInkGroup.com

info@FreshInkGroup.com

Twitter: @FreshInkGroup

Facebook.com/FreshInkGroup

LinkedIn: Fresh Ink Group

Also by George Dismukes!

She was forced to stand alone against a danger that no one would believe existed. Not just once. The problem was, she didn't know when the horror would end, because every time she thought it was over, it started again!

Angie Holland thought she was through with Belize forever. But a TV news report about the mysterious disappearance of several scuba divers at the Great Blue Hole sent chills up her spine. As much as the tried to reject the idea, in her heart, she knew the job was not finished. She thought the siren was dead! She had followed the formula precisely to make sure that Maris had been dispatched. Every instruction, including use of the obsidian dagger, had been followed to the letter. Now, it seemed like a recurring bad dream, the bitch was back!

Or was she? There is no way that Maris could have survived. Several people, including Angie had seen her dissolve into a pile of ashes. Could this new havoc be brought on by her equally evil sister? There was only one way to find out, and only one person to do it. Angie picked up the phone and made reservations for the quickest flight to Belize.

Also by George Dismukes!

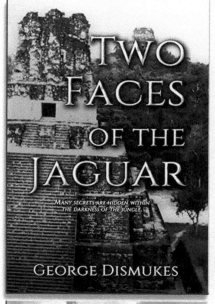

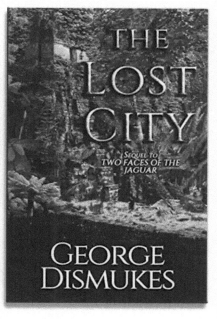

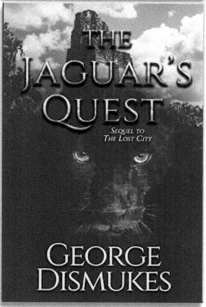

Many secrets are hidden within the darkness of the jungle. Behold this trilogy about a man, a woman, a black jaguar, and an ancient Mayan legend.

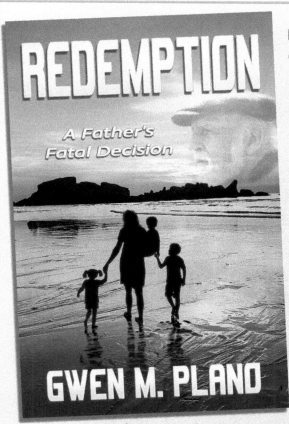

REDEMPTION

A Father's Fatal Decision

GWEN M. PLANO

Family secrets can be deadly. When Lisa visits her parents one fateful Saturday morning, she hugs her father and takes her suitcase to her childhood bedroom. The doorbell rings, and one minute later, her father lies dead on the floor— three bullets to the chest. The death of Eric Holmes sends shockwaves throughout the quiet neighbor- hood. But for the Holmes family, it is devastating. In this fast-paced psychological thriller, Lisa and her brother embark on a quest to solve the mystery of their father's murder. The journey takes them into a secret world where nothing is as it seems. Once the puzzle pieces begin to coalesce, they realize that their father had multiple lives. As the facts unravel, the siblings discover the true meaning of *Redemption*.

Fresh Ink Group
FreshInkGroup.com

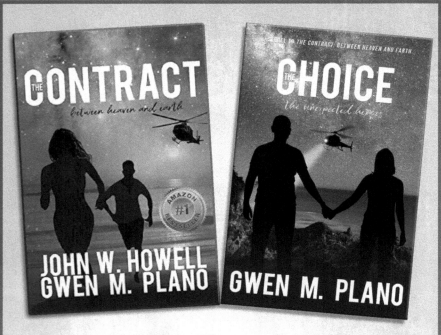

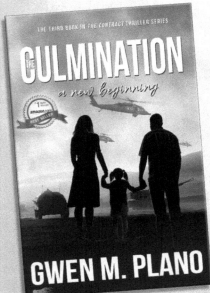

Paranormal,
Romantic,
Spiritual
Thriller
Trilogy!

FreshInkGroup.com

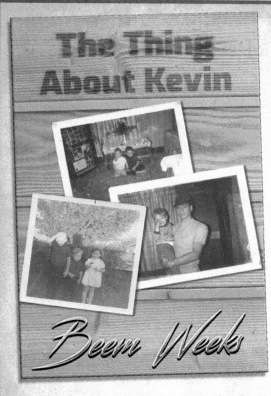

Milton Keynes UK
Ingram Content Group UK Ltd.
UKHW020135220823
427215UK00015B/891